P9-DHT-744

# Genevieve's War

CHARLESTON COUNTY LIBRARY

# Genevieve's War

## PATRICIA REILLY GIFF

*Holiday House / New York*

Text copyright © 2017 by Patricia Reilly Giff
Illustrations copyright © 2017 by Becca Stadtlander
All Rights Reserved

HOLIDAY HOUSE is registered in the U.S. Patent and Trademark Office.
Printed and bound in January 2019 at Maple Press, York, PA, USA.
5 7 9 10 8 6 4
www.holidayhouse.com
Library of Congress Cataloging-in-Publication Data

Names: Giff, Patricia Reilly.
Title: Genevieve's war / by Patricia Reilly Giff.
Description: First edition. | New York : Holiday House, [2017] | Summary:
"In August 1939 Genevieve makes an impulsive decision not to get on the train
to take her by boat back to New York and must spend the duration of
World War II with her grandmother in a small village in Alsace, France,
where she becomes involved with the French resistance."—Provided by publisher.
Identifiers: LCCN 2016027038 | ISBN 9780823438006 (hardcover)
Subjects: | CYAC: World War, 1939–1945—Underground
Movements—France—Fiction. | Grandparent and child—Fiction.
Self-reliance—Fiction. | France—History—German occupation,
1940–1945—Fiction.
Classification: LCC PZ7.G3626 Ge 2017 | DDC [Fic]—dc23
LC record available at https://lccn.loc.gov/2016027038

ISBN 978-0-8234-4178-5 (paperback)

*For George Nicholson, beloved friend.*

*For James Matthew Giff, beloved son.*

# Alsace, France

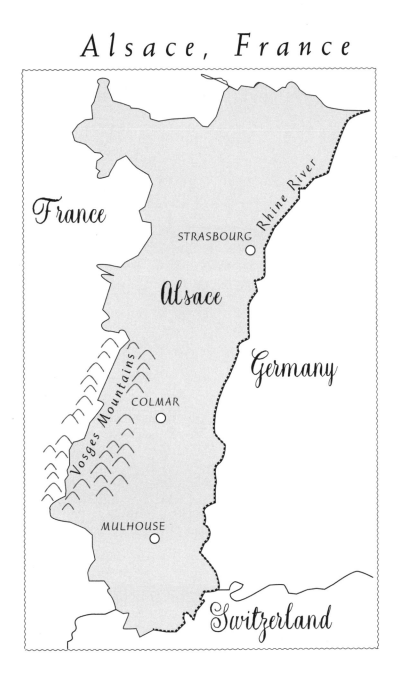

France

Rhine River

STRASBOURG

Alsace

Germany

Vosges Mountains

COLMAR

MULHOUSE

Switzerland

# THE END

My heart drummed against my chest, my throat so dry I couldn't swallow.

Mémé and I crouched on the dirt floor of the farm-house cellar, our dog, Louis, huddled beside us. The sounds of the mortar and bursts of artillery seemed to go on forever. We were trapped in the middle: the Americans on one side of us, the Germans on the other.

It was freezing without heat, and dark! I'd burned our only candle down to a nub; then it had sputtered and died.

"I have to go upstairs," I told Mémé. "We need quilts and sweaters."

I felt her reach out. "Don't, Genevieve. I'll go."

My grandmother, braver than I!

"It's all right." I stood and ran my hands along the wall to find my way to the stairs.

A tremendous boom. The house shook.

We knew the cellar was the safest place in the bombardment, but suppose the house came down? We'd be buried under stone and timber with no one to help us.

Was that happening right now to the shops in the

village, the school, the farmhouses along the way? I stumbled over something that rolled and clattered, and then I went up into the daylight, blinking.

Everything looked so normal. I passed the hall table with my father's picture, the living room chairs.

But nothing was normal. In the kitchen, windows were shattered; shards of glass that must have been a hundred years old covered the wide sills. My feet crunched against pieces on the stone floor.

The three-colored cat, half hidden under the table, peered out at me. She hissed when I tried to pick her up, and backed away. Poor thing, as frightened as we were. I'd have to leave her for now.

Another boom.

No time!

I yanked open the drawer for candles, glancing outside quickly. The gravel driveway was torn up, a tree split, the winter fields gray with patches of snow.

Head down, the candles in my pocket, I ran to pull the quilt off the bed, sweaters off hooks, the sounds of the battle so much louder than they had been in the cellar.

I threw the quilt and sweaters down the stairs to

*free my hands. Then I lighted a candle with shaking fingers as the cat dived ahead of me.*

*Who'd said the war would be over someday?*

*We'd all said it! It would be over and there'd be peace.*

*Someday would never come.*

# BEFORE

# one

"*Gen?*" André's voice was loud.

I leaned over the hall table to peer out the window; one elbow knocked my father's picture to the floor.

André beckoned from the barn. "Look what I found. Hurry."

I put the picture back on the table, wiping off imaginary dust with one sleeve. Who was he anyway, my father with his grim face, his hands balled into fists?

My wooden sabots clattered on the stone floor as I sped through the kitchen.

"Don't slam—" Mémé began over her shoulder.

I caught the door just in time, hopped over the three-colored cat on the stone step, then crossed the gravel path to the barn, with its sweet smell of hay.

Inside, André pointed: two ancient bicycles leaned against each other in one of the stalls. Bits of hay covered the seats and cobwebs stretched across the spokes.

Bicycles! We could pump the tires with air and ride away from the farm, pedaling up one hill and coasting down the next, arms out. I smiled, remembering when André had taught me to ride. *"You'll speed along as if you've been doing this forever, Gen,"* he'd said.

For the first time in days, I'd stop thinking of him sailing home to New York, leaving me with our disagreeable grandmother, Mémé, to weed rows of cabbages and pick bugs off the beans, to speak Alsatian or French every minute, and never hear a word in English.

I'd be here for another two weeks!

And then, home. But not to Aunt Marie, not to our house in Springfield Gardens, not to my old school in September. I brushed my hair away, determined to brush my thoughts away too.

André was filling the tires, so I wiped off a few dried spiders, as old as the bikes. Then, zigzagging along the path, the gravel spitting out from under the wheels, we called to Mémé. "Going for a ride."

We didn't wait to hear what she'd say.

We flew! André led the way, going east, past farms and woods filled with evergreens.

Someone was yelling at us!

I glanced over my shoulder and slowed down. Rémy, younger than André, a couple of years older than me, pedaled toward us, waving.

Rémy had been the best part of this summer. Rémy with blue eyes and curly hair! Rémy who towered over me and made my heart beat faster!

"Some bikes!" he called.

His wasn't much better; I had to laugh. "Race you to the top of the hill," I called back.

André pulled to one side, watching. I rode past with Rémy behind me, letting me win.

André caught up, and later, we stopped at a grassy meadow to see an ancient stone tower. A messy storks' nest rested precariously on top. "The white storks of Alsace," André said. "With long legs like yours, Gen."

Rémy grinned at me, a tiny scar at the corner of his mouth dimpling. He made me smile too. If only he lived in New York!

I shaded my eyes to see the mother bird's head and a hint of her folded black wings, but her babies were hidden deep in the nest.

"If I were here this winter," André said, "I'd climb the tower and see the world."

Rémy said, "Sure," and I sputtered, "Really!"

But André could do almost anything. He was my best friend and a great cook. Now he was going home ahead of me. He'd spent the summer here working in the village bistro. Last summer he'd been in Basel, the summer before in Strasbourg and Colmar, working in restaurants. Now he'd study business in college so he could open his own restaurant someday. "I'll call it Genevieve's Place," he always said. "And you'll be the star."

"Some star, with skinny brown braids," I always said.

But now, I bit my lip: my brother, skinny, with coal-black hair, leaving. André, who laughed at everything, who cared about me.

He read my mind. "I'll visit you at Cousin Ellen's. And I'll bring you a red parasol to make you happy." He stopped when he saw my face. He knew what I was thinking. Cousin Ellen! My mother's friend. I hardly knew her.

Aunt Marie, my mother as long as I could remember, was teaching in Canada, so far north that even letters would be hard to get.

*No choice,* she'd said, *I have to work in this little*

*village for the book I'm writing. It'll make all the differ-
ence to us. But we'll be together by Christmas, I promise.*

Did I say something aloud? Rémy looked at me with sympathy. "Don't go back, Gen. Stay."

Stay with Mémé, who complained about everything? I shook my head.

We rode along and passed a half-timbered house, a chestnut tree shading its windows. It was blue-gray, a beautiful color. Then a farm filled with vegetables and plum trees. Rémy pointed. "I wish it were mine," he said. "Someday I'll farm."

"What about your parents' pharmacy?" André asked.

Rémy grinned. "I'll leave that to my little sister, Céline. She's three. On her way to growing up."

We stopped too far away from the Rhine to see the water, but I knew it was there. And beyond that, Germany!

"They're coming, Gen," Rémy said. "The Germans will run right over us."

I felt a quick tightening in my chest. André's face was serious. "They want to take Alsace back and gobble up the rest of Europe."

He reached over and touched my hand on the

handlebar. "You'll get out before they come." He frowned. I knew he was thinking about our father and grandparents, who were born here. "I hate to desert Mémé," he said.

I thought of her stern face, the lines that crisscrossed her forehead. Born in 1876, she was in her sixties but seemed like a hundred. And what I knew of my father would fit in a thimble. I thought of his picture: Gérard Michel, a stern man glaring into the camera.

I didn't care one bit that we were leaving Mémé and Alsace. It couldn't be soon enough for me.

At that moment, the sky turned from blue to charcoal gray. Lightning streaked across the sky and a clap of thunder followed. "Let's go!" Rémy shouted.

Rain beat on our heads and shoulders. Heads down, we pedaled along the way we'd come. At last, Mémé's farm was ahead of us. We waved as Rémy kept going toward his parents' pharmacy in the village square.

We were soaked, our clothes dripping. We wheeled the bicycles into the barn, dried them off, and covered them with old drop cloths, and again, I thought of André leaving.

I put my hand on his arm, but before I could say anything, he glanced toward the kitchen window, where

Mémé stared out at the rain. "She'll be alone without us," he said.

"She's been alone for years. She'll be glad when I'm gone."

And I'd be glad too, more than glad.

# *two*

@Mémé and I pulled weeds, our nails broken and lined with soil. How strong I'd become this summer. In the field, at first, my face had blistered, but then I tanned until I could spend long hours in the sun. My arms and legs had new muscles.

Mémé stretched, one hand rubbing her back. "The Germans are coming soon," she said, almost echoing André's words before he'd left, hugging me to him.

"But not yet."

And not for me. I'd be on the *Normandie* traveling west. At the railing, I'd watch the rolling sea, and in the dining room, I'd order petits fours thick with fondant icing.

If only I hadn't dreamed about Cousin Ellen last night. She was kind and friendly and when Aunt Marie asked if I could stay with her, she'd said, *"I'd love it."*

But I wouldn't know one person in Flushing, wouldn't have one friend, instead of being home in Springfield Gardens, where I knew everyone. Now I'd even be leaving my new friend, Katrin, who lived on the next farm, the best friend I'd ever had.

And Rémy. Oh, Rémy!

This was my last day. My ticket lay on the edge of the bed upstairs. Madame Thierry, who was a neighbor at home, and almost as old as Mémé, would meet me at the train station.

*"You can't go alone,"* Aunt Marie had said in June after André had left, her face worried. *"Madame Thierry is going to Alsace for the summer too. She'll take care of you both ways."*

I had to smile. Madame Thierry was the one who needed care!

"You have less than an hour," Mémé said. "This ship may be the last to cross before the war. If you miss the train you may not reach it in time."

War! That was all anyone talked about. "Less than an hour," I repeated to Mémé, as if it didn't matter one way or the other. I could be as tough as this old woman, who, bent and limping, still managed to run the farm alone.

Lines pleated themselves above her lips. "Finish packing, Genevieve. We'll take the cart to the railroad station. Your holiday is over."

Holiday. I pursed my lips the way she did. Holiday was Jones Beach on Long Island, the waves smashing onto the shore. It wasn't digging in Mémé's fields, all the way across the Atlantic, stuffing sausages, or boiling jars to hold beans and plums.

It certainly wasn't sleeping in the upstairs bedroom where my father had spent his childhood. The ceiling sloped low over my head, and the straw mattress crackled when I moved.

Most of all, it wasn't spending a summer with Mémé.

But what had Aunt Marie said? *"You and André know about your mother, but what about your father? Your grandmother? The farm that will be yours someday?"*

She'd told me that she and my mother had gone to Alsace, that Mom had seen my father in the village. *The two of us with French parents, able to speak French ourselves,* she'd said. *Your mother fell in love.*

I knew so much about my mother. She'd been skinny like André and tall like me. She wore Evening in Paris perfume and loved to dance with me in her arms.

I could almost see her.

But all I could see of my father was a face that looked as if he'd eaten a lemon!

How different everything would have been if they hadn't taken the train to the mountains when I was a baby. If the train hadn't jumped the tracks. If they still lived.

I threw a bunch of weeds toward the wheelbarrow but missed. Mémé muttered something behind me. *Clumsiness,* probably. I had a quick thought of Aunt Marie, who called me Flyaway Girl. *Things just fly away from you and are lost,* she'd say, and laugh.

I walked across the field, wanting to dance across. *Last time,* I told myself. Dozens of cabbages would be ready to harvest soon. But not by me!

The three-colored cat was sunning herself on the path; she reached out with one paw to give me a little scratch as I passed.

Inside, I trailed my fingers over the massive kitchen table. The room was dark, with a huge fireplace; copper pots hung on hooks, and vegetables simmered on the stove, almost ready for the jars on the counter. A crusty loaf of bread covered with a tea towel was on the table, and I cut myself a slice to munch on.

Louis, the shepherd dog, padded in behind me.

"He's a watchdog," Mémé had told me a dozen times. "Meant to be kept outside at night."

I'd forgotten to close the door again, but it wasn't night! I bent to hug him, his rough fur against my cheek. "Good dog." I slipped him a chunk of bread too.

After I walked him outside, I climbed the stairs, my hand raised over the banister, which bristled with splinters, and scooped up one of my knee socks from the top step.

It didn't take long to fold everything into my suitcase: underwear and socks, skirts and blouses. I stared at the books I'd brought with me. I'd read them over and over, myths and folktales, and a French book about a lost dog, from my friend, Katrin. Aunt Marie, who loved to read, had taught me to read too, when I was only three. I'd have to carry the books in the string bag I'd made this summer, a bit of a mess.

I changed into Sunday clothes, sliding into patent leather shoes and leaving the wooden sabots under the bed.

Did I have everything? The dresser drawers were warped and so hard to open that I hadn't used them. But just in case, I checked.

They were empty, except for the bottom one. It held an old photo of Mémé. How pretty she'd been, young and smiling a little. How different from the sour old woman she was now. I turned the picture over. *Miel* was written on the back. Honey! More like vinegar, if you asked me.

No one would have written *Miel* on the back of my father's picture.

I pulled my things down the stairs and outside.

Sister, the horse, was tethered to the cart. I rested my hand on her chocolate side. Her skin rippled under my hand, and she looked back at me as if she knew I was leaving. Mémé stood on the other side of the cart, leaning against it. A surprise. She never leaned against anything.

*"The poor horse doesn't even have a name yet,"* André had said in June. *"How old is she, Mémé?"*

*"Twelve."*

*"I christen her Sister,"* he'd said, *"in honor of my sister."*

*"Me?"*

*"Her legs are long. And her huge brown eyes are like yours."*

*"Mine are gray."*

He'd grinned. "Doesn't matter. Her feet clop just like yours."

I'd looked quickly at Mémé, at her faint smile. No one could resist André.

I gave the horse another pat. I'd miss her and all the animals, even the cow André had named Elsie. "Elsie?" Mémé had echoed.

He'd laughed. "It's a cow's name."

"An American cow," I'd added.

What would happen if I dashed into the barn and said good-bye to the cow, or to the hens that pecked at seed in their pen?

But Mémé was frowning, impatient. No detours!

Her lips chewed on themselves as she stared at the side field with its rows of squash, and beyond them the potato plants with their purple flowers.

Did she care that I was leaving? That she'd be alone this fall, to pull all that from the earth, to fill dozens of jars of food, and store potatoes and apples in the cool cellar? Only one person would eat them all winter.

Louis circled the cart, wanting to come with us. I ran my hand over his head and kissed his gray muzzle. "I'll miss you," I whispered. I climbed up, but Mémé still stood on the other side of the cart.

I saw then how pale she was, her wrinkled face dotted with perspiration.

"What is it?" I asked.

"Nothing." She held on to the edge of the cart as she climbed up slowly, dragging her left foot.

"What?" I asked again.

"It's just twisted . . . ," she began, and didn't finish.

I looked down and saw a line of blood on the hem of her long dress.

"How did you do this?"

"Stop, Genevieve. We'll miss the train with all your questions."

She flicked the reins lightly on Sister's back. Then we were on our way, leaving the house with its red shutters, the cow, the chickens, the pig, the three-colored cat and Louis, whose thick tail wagged uncertainly.

# three

*Cypress* trees lined the road on each side of us. Sister's bells jangled, and with every step she took, I heard, *Summer's over.*

Nearby, the woodcutter was sawing in the forest. Sometimes I'd caught a glimpse of him, straps over his bent shoulders, pulling his cart along, with new wood piled high. He'd raise his hand in a gentle wave, then duck his head.

We passed the Moellers' farmhouse, where Katrin leaned against the window, waving. Yesterday we'd said a long good-bye, crying a little, hugging, promising to write and to be friends forever.

Katrin was funny and warm. Her cheeks were round and covered with freckles, and her hair was a halo of curls. She never stopped talking ... some of it about America, and all of it mixed up. She'd lean forward:

*"Do you see cowboys in New York City all the time?"* Or *"How about buffaloes? If I'm going to be a writer, I have to know these things."*

I looked back over my shoulder until she and the farm disappeared at the turn of the road.

Next to me, Mémé faced straight ahead, her lips in a thin line, her jaws clenched. What had she done to her foot?

We made our way into the village square. Baskets of red and white geraniums were everywhere. Shop doors and windows in the upstairs apartments were open against the heat.

Three old men in berets sat at a table in front of the bistro. They'd been in the same spot every day since I'd come, voices raised, arguing over one thing or another.

"Let's stop at the pâtisserie," I said.

Mémé twitched one narrow shoulder, as if she were asking why.

"I want to say good-bye."

She pulled on the reins, and I tumbled out of the cart before she could change her mind.

Inside the pâtisserie, I breathed in the smell of plum tarts baking in the oven. My mouth watered as I glanced at shelves filled with cakes and éclairs plump with whipped cream.

Madame Jacques wiped her floury hands on her apron and reached into the case for a meringue for me. "My favorite," I said.

"Ah yes. Your father's favorite too."

He loved meringues? My father with his grim face?

"So, Genevieve." Madame Jacques wiped her warm face, her cheeks like soft dough. "Summer is over, and you leave before the Germans come."

I nodded, the sweet meringue melting on my tongue.

She tilted her head. "I think you will come back. Maybe not soon. It will be a long time." She tapped the wooden floor with one foot. "The Germans remember that Alsace belonged to them once. They want us back."

She smiled then. "My son, Claude, is still sleeping upstairs. Lazy boy. Otherwise he'd say good-bye to you too."

From the window, I saw Mémé frowning at me. Madame Jacques gave me a kiss on each cheek. I went out the door and was barely onto the cart when Mémé snapped the reins again and the horse jolted forward.

On the other side of the square, Monsieur Philippe lounged in the doorway of his shop, books piled up in the small window next to him. He looked at me impassively. His lips were impossibly thick, his teeth nut brown. He was nothing like Madame Jacques, who laughed at everything, touching your shoulder as she did.

As we passed the pharmacy, Rémy stood at the open door. He mouthed something. Was it *I will miss you?* Did he look sad, thinking we wouldn't see each other for a long time?

As the horse labored up the hill, I looked back at the fairy-tale village. The houses were half-timbered, their stone walls painted yellow or pink, or green and the church steeple rose above all of it in a thin point.

I remembered the ancient stone tower with its messy storks' nest. *I hate to desert Mémé,* André had said. Did I say it aloud? She turned to stare at me sharply, but I pretended to glance at the field. We didn't speak for the rest of the way.

At the station, I pulled out my suitcase and the string bag of books. I tucked my purse under my arm, wondering where I'd left my gloves. I jumped down, and with my hand gentling Sister's back, I glanced at

Mémé. "Thank you," I managed. What else could I say? "The farm is beautiful." I realized it was true: the field in the morning, green and washed, the Vosges Mountains in the distance.

She leaned forward. "You may come again after the war, Genevieve."

I blinked in surprise, then glanced down. Her foot turned in and there was a drop of blood on her sock. But before I could say a word, she was turning the cart on her way back to the farm.

# four

*Dust* rose from the cart. I watched until Sister trotted around a curve; then I dragged my heavy suitcase and the books into the station.

Inside, the wooden benches were filled. People leaned against the walls or sat on the cement floor, boxes and bags at their feet. A buzz of voices rose and fell like angry bees.

The four Grossmans, a Jewish family, the mother and father and two children, were pressed together in a far corner. Katrin had told me they were leaving for safety. How terrible that the Germans hated them. And why? I waved but they didn't see me.

Madame Thierry sat on a bench, eyes closed, mouth opened, asleep.

I stood nearby, next to a stanchion. The ceiling was

open to the sky; pigeons flew back and forth, wings whirring, feathers drifting. A cloud changed shapes: an old man, an angel's wing, a giant shoe.

I closed my eyes. *The train to Le Havre, the ship. Then New York. The library, black-and-white ice cream sodas with Aunt Marie!* I swallowed. No! I'd have to find another library near Ellen, Aunt Marie would be far away, and André wouldn't be scrambling eggs on Saturday mornings. *Gen, you're my best customer!*

Next to me, a woman was eating a buttery crêpe. It was folded in four, and sugar dotted her dress. My mouth watered. I had a few francs left, so I went to find one at the shop.

I returned to my place, a warm crêpe in my hand. Katrin had taught me to make crêpes, but she was so busy talking she'd burned the first two. If only she lived in New York. Ah, Katrin!

And Rémy.

I brought the crêpe to my mouth; I smelled the butter, but I didn't taste it.

*The first snow in New York. Christmas! Aunt Marie would be home by then, and André for the holidays. And I'd be there.*

A family sat on the bench next to Madame Thierry, surrounded by packages and even an empty birdcage. The man's feet rested on a metal trunk. Their daughter, maybe five years old, inched her way closer, her eyes on my crêpe. She held out her hand, but her mother reached for her. *"Non."*

"It's all right," I said, smiling at the little girl.

The mother leaned down toward her. "She's saving her crêpe for later."

Why couldn't I eat it?

I heard the chug of the train, the shrill whistle. People rushed for bags, for trunks. Someone called, "Where are you, Charles? Hurry."

I tapped Madame Thierry on the shoulder. "Time to go."

She jumped. "I've been looking all over for you."

Sure! "Sorry," I said as I helped her to her feet.

The train pulled in, and pigeons flew up, feathers floating.

I remembered leaving Katrin. *"I've always wanted to see a buffalo. I'm going to write books,"* she'd said. *"Tons of them."*

And Rémy: *"Don't go back, Gen."*

But Mémé!

How had she managed to hurt herself before I left? I didn't love her. I didn't even like her. I felt a stab of anger. But could she have broken a bone? That miserable woman would have to harvest the beans, the squash, the cabbages by herself. But suppose she couldn't do all that? What would she eat this winter? I ran one hand over my arm, summer muscles.

Ridiculous.

Suppose there really was a war? I shivered. Maybe, maybe not.

Why didn't I hurry? Why didn't I take those steps as the train door opened?

Aunt Marie! *"It's not always thinking of being happy. Doing the right thing will make you happy."*

I handed my crêpe to the little girl, the lump in my throat choking me.

The train began to fill and the platform emptied. Madame Thierry walked ahead.

*Still time.*

"Genevieve?" she called.

I waved. "Go ahead. I can't..."

She didn't wait to hear the rest. Shaking her head, she stepped onto the train. The doors were closing.

*Grab everything,* I told myself. *Run!* I didn't do that; I stood still.

The train began to move slowly, to pick up speed. I put my arms around the stanchion as if it were alive, as if it could comfort me.

# five

*How* could I take that endless walk back to the farm?

*Folle,* Mémé would say. *Crazy.*

The sun beat on my head as I dragged everything along. At the top of a hill, I moved aside as a cart lumbered by. If only I'd spent those francs on something to drink.

I'd have to leave the suitcase and the books, but not where anyone could see. I walked farther and found a spot for them in a wooded area, dotted with evergreens. I'd come back tomorrow with Sister and the cart.

I sank down next to an old tree and leaned my forehead against the bark. I saw Aunt Marie's face, her small glasses framing her blue eyes, her dark hair in a pageboy.

One day when I was little, I'd noticed our glass

doorknobs. *"Diamonds,"* I'd whispered. *"We must be rich."* Aunt Marie had put her warm arms around me. *"Any house is rich if you're in it,"* she'd said.

What would Aunt Marie think when she found out what I'd done? *The right thing!*

What would André think?

I walked farther into the woods and sat on a fallen tree trunk. My sobs were so loud that anyone coming along the road might have heard me. I wept until there were no tears left; then I left the suitcase and the string bag with the books under a patch of thick bushes.

I walked for what seemed forever, my feet blistering in the stiff patent leather shoes, the comfortable ones still inside the suitcase.

I passed the school and reached the village square, hurrying now. The shops were closed except for the bistro, where André had spent most of the summer chopping onions and carrots, washing endless dishes, and loving it all. The old men still sat in front, heads together, arguing.

Rémy opened the pharmacy door. "Gen?" In two quick steps he was standing next to me, reaching out to hug me.

For just that second I felt a burst of happiness.

"But the Germans—" he began.

The war! "I have to go." I could hardly talk.

"I'm sorry," he said. "I'm so sorry."

I nodded, then turned and kept walking. From the last hill I saw the tile roof of Katrin's farmhouse. A moment later, she came down the path, arms out. "What happened, Genevieve? Why—"

I held up my hand, out of breath. She led me toward her house. Her brother, Karl, poked his head out the door and smiled. Her mother was shelling beans at the table, her head turned, talking to someone in the next room. Were they speaking German? She looked up. "Genevieve!"

Katrin poured milk for me and I drank it leaning against the counter, gulping it down. "Thank you," I managed when the glass was almost empty.

"Why, Gen?" Katrin began, but I just shook my head. She danced around the table. "I'm so glad you stayed. I'll put you in the first book I write. In the meantime, we'll celebrate the fall together."

I was filled with homesickness, but when I listened to her, I felt better. I held the cool glass up to my hot forehead, then drank the rest.

The church bells chimed the Angelus.

Six o'clock!

I jumped up. "I have to go. But thank you for the milk." I backed out the door. Mémé might be sitting at the kitchen table, a thick stew in front of her, Sunday's leftover chicken shredded into it, with a handful of juniper berries for flavor.

What would she say?

I went along the road until her farm was in front of me: the house with the pointed roof, the barn, Sister in the field, the filthy pig rooting nearby.

Louis barked, his tail thumping, telling Mémé I was home. I knelt down beside him, my head on his, my arms around his thick fur. I hopped over the three-colored cat on the step, then went inside.

Mémé wasn't at the table. She was stretched out on the long bench next to the hearth, her foot raised. When she saw me, her hand went to her mouth, my long-dead grandfather Victor's ring loose on her finger.

I sank onto a chair, easing off my Sunday shoes, wiggling my toes in the heavy stockings.

"What are you doing here?" She almost bit off the words.

What could I say? "Your ankle?" I asked.

"You've missed the train, the ship. Headlong! Do you ever think?"

The tears in my eyes were tears of rage. "I came back to—"

"Help me?" She blew air between her lips.

I wouldn't give her the satisfaction. "No!"

"All that money for tickets," she said. "Wasted!"

I caught my breath. Aunt Marie saving money for months, all for my trip. But not for André. He'd used his restaurant money. Why hadn't I remembered that? I felt sick to my stomach.

I stamped over to the hearth and heated two bowls of chicken stew. I sawed off two slabs of bread and brought hers over to the small table next to the couch.

"You'll have to write to the cousin," Mémé said, not touching the stew.

I wanted to cover my ears. I slammed my bowl down on the large table. I sat with my back toward her, so I couldn't see her angry face, and spooned in the salty stew, suddenly not hungry.

"A disruption in my life," I thought I heard her whisper.

At home, André cooked every Sunday, thick beef

stews in the winter, cold tomato soups on hot summer days. We'd sit around the kitchen table, the three of us, talking, laughing.

I had to stop thinking of it. I couldn't let myself cry again. I left the kitchen a little later, seeing that Mémé hadn't touched her food.

Upstairs, I threw myself on the bed. A piece of straw poked through the mattress, and I pulled it out. At home every night, I'd hear the mournful wail of the Long Island train as it passed the Higbie Avenue station. I'd cuddle deeper under the covers, cozy and warm.

André would have put his arms around me and told me not to cry. *Everything will be all right,* he'd have said.

But it wouldn't be all right. I turned my head into the musty pillow. I'd made a terrible mistake.

# six

$\mathfrak{It}$ was barely light when I threw on a dress I'd forgotten to pack and scrambled under the bed for the wooden sabots. No more feeling sorry for myself! No more thinking about the ship sailing west. There was nothing I could do about it but write to Cousin Ellen. I'd tell her I was staying in Alsace. I'd say that Aunt Marie would be happy that I'd be with my dear grandmother. *Dear grandmother.* Such a lie!

I'd write to Aunt Marie too, a letter that would stay in the mailbox at home for months. I'd remind her of doing the right thing. I'd promise we'd be together by Christmas. After all, how long could a war last? A couple of weeks? A month or two?

André's note would be easy. He always understood everything, so I'd barely have to explain.

Louis lay on the rag rug, his dark eyes following me as I moved around the room. "Oh, Louis," I said. "I forgot to put you out last night." I was glad, though. I was beginning to love this dog!

We went down the narrow stairs together. No matter how early I'd been up all summer, Mémé was always awake, dressed, her hair in a tight bun. Elsie would be tethered out back, already milked. Sister would be frolicking in the field after her quiet night in the barn, and the pig would be wandering around, snuffling and snorting.

But not this morning. Mémé still hadn't moved from the bench, and the stew had congealed in the bowl.

"You can't lie there forever," I said, ready to ask how I could help her.

"You're thirteen years old. Don't tell me what to do."

Impossible.

I tried again. "Can I get you something for your ankle?"

She stared out the window. "The animals," she said. "The horse, the cow . . ."

I nodded. "Do you need a doctor?"

She shook her head. "It will heal by itself."

I grabbed a chunk of bread, slathered it with jam and went outside. The three-colored cat stared up at me with her great yellow eyes. I grinned at her. "Not too friendly, I see, but how about a quick pat?"

I reached out, but she was having none of my friendship. Claws unsheathed, she raked my hand.

"Next time," I said over my shoulder, and hurried to the barn. I gave Sister her oats and scattered seed for the chickens. Slop went into the pig trough, and I managed to milk the cow. I wouldn't have known how to do any of it early this summer. Still it took half the morning.

"Genevieve," Katrin called, and trudged up the gravel path.

I went to meet her and we sat on the stone steps outside the kitchen door.

"My poor friend," she said, her face earnest. "You're the best person I know. Staying here for that old woman."

I glanced back at the window. Had Mémé heard?

But Katrin was on to something else. "Wait until you see Monsieur Henri, the history teacher. He's in love with himself and his swept-back hair."

School! I'd forgotten that too. New teachers, new kids.

"You'll have to learn German," Katrin said.

I shook my head. Aunt Marie was a language

teacher. At home, she spoke French to us one day, Alsatian another, and sometimes, she threw in an afternoon of German. I'd have no problem with that.

"*Guten Morgen,*" Katrin said. "Know what that means?"

"Good morning. I'm not a complete idiot." Then it came to me. My clothes. My books. How had I forgotten them? I scrambled up.

"What?" Katrin asked.

"I left my things..." I hurried along the driveway and burst into the kitchen. Mémé was up, leaning against the table.

"Could I take the cart?" I rushed through the rest of it: my heavy suitcase, the string bag, the woods.

"Go ahead," Mémé said, and under her breath, "Why am I not surprised?"

In the barn, I harnessed Sister to the cart. Imagine Aunt Marie seeing me do that! Before I came to Alsace, I'd never seen a horse or cart up close, much less a harness.

We came around the driveway, and Katrin climbed up next to me. "We'll drive toward the railroad station," I told her.

As we passed the village, Madame Jacques was at

the pâtisserie window, shocked to see me. She raised her hand to wave.

Katrin and I searched, staring at trees, at bushes, climbing off the cart and wandering through the woods. But as the sun went down, we had to give up.

Mémé had managed to put a plate of cheese on the table, with cold sausages and bread. She was sitting at the table. We ate silently, but then I began, the words almost forced out of my mouth. "I have nothing else to wear, Mémé."

"You didn't find your suitcase." Mémé chewed on her lips, a miserable habit, especially since I'd noticed I did the same thing. "I've resigned myself. You are head-strong and forgetful, and I will have to live with that."

It was unbearable to think that I was one bit like her. "I'm not," I blurted.

Mémé raised wispy eyebrows and motioned to me to help her take the steps to her bedroom upstairs. I opened the door thinking the room reminded me of her, everything neat, the quilt soldier-straight. Only the coral necklace looped across the top of her dresser seemed out of place.

Mémé sank down in the chair next to the window,

and I saw then that she'd managed to wrap a cloth around her ankle.

Across the room where she must have seen it every morning was a painting. I knew nothing about art, but I could see how beautiful it was. I couldn't stop staring at it: two girls wearing red skirts, blouses with puffy white sleeves, and huge black bows in their hair. They stood in a field, with woven baskets of plums in their arms; the light from a late-afternoon sun streamed over their shoulders.

I wanted to stand there and drink it in forever. "The painting," I breathed.

"I'm on the right, an old friend on the left. Gérard always laughed at the bows."

I couldn't believe it: that beautiful girl, her soft dark hair flowing under the bow, her smooth hands grasping the basket. *Miel. Honey.* And my father laughed? A surprise!

"Open the armoire door," she said. Dresses hung in a row, shoes marched along underneath. "Choose."

I shook my head. "Whatever you want to give me."

"Humility doesn't become you."

I took a thick knitted sweater off the top shelf, then

slipped two dresses from their hangers. She had sewn them by hand, as she had all her clothing. Her stitches were tiny and even, not like my own when I had to make an apron in school last year. "Mile-long stitches wandering all over the fabric," Mrs. Rizzo, the sewing teacher, had sniffed.

"Ah, something else," Mémé said. "I'd forgotten about this. Gérard's notebook is there too. Take it."

"I'm really sorry," I said. If only she'd say she was grateful I'd stayed. "Please tell me what you did to your ankle."

She hesitated. "A fall in the field. It will heal." She pointed to the dresser. "Underwear in the drawer."

I took a couple of pairs, bleached and clean, fit for a woman over sixty.

"I'll just stay here now," she said, so I bundled everything in my arms and nodded thanks.

She held up her hand. "It's all right."

I knew it wasn't all right, but I kept going down the hall and into my bedroom.

I sat on the bed, the straw crackling, to open the notebook. What could that grim-faced man have written? But maybe not a man! Maybe a boy who liked meringues and laughed over huge bows!

As I opened the book, I saw that he wasn't a very good student. Pages were marked with the teacher's red pencil: *poor, terrible work, Gérard, be more careful.*

In the back, doodles! And on the last page, he'd drawn a picture of a girl with loopy curls and a long, skinny neck. There was a big X over her. *Suzanne talks too much. She tells the teacher everything.*

I had to smile. My father's notebook was just like mine when I was in third or fourth grade. His Suzanne was just like Ruthie, a girl in my class whose hand was raised every two minutes to tattle on someone.

I fell asleep wondering if Suzanne, grown-up now, still lived in Alsace, and trying not to think about home.

# WAR

# seven

*Every* day I waited for mail. Still nothing from André. He hated to write, I knew that from summers before. And when he did write, his letters were short and ... "Useless," I'd told him.

Mémé spent most of her time at the kitchen table, and when she walked outside, I could see what an effort it took. I was beginning to realize how frail she was.

"You'll need socks," she said, unraveling the wool from old socks and knitting new ones.

Managing the animals was becoming easier. I loved the smell of hay in the barn, Elsie looking back at me as I milked her, and the hens clucking in their pen. I learned how to hang the herbs from the small garden on hooks so they'd dry. The kitchen smelled of thyme, and rosemary, and dill.

One morning, when I came downstairs, Mémé was

listening to the radio play the French national anthem. She looked up, her bony fingers knotted together, gray wool on the table in front of her. "We're at war." She stared at me. "You know now what you've done."

I raised my chin, but I couldn't think of anything to say.

News of the soldiers fighting farther west came during the next few days. The Germans had barreled through the massive trenches the French had built, and even gone around them in their tanks and jeeps. Everyone along the German border was evacuated for safety, and we were all given gas masks.

I was afraid, but Mémé said only, "We're lucky to be five miles from the border. I couldn't bear to leave the farm."

That fall was chilly, with drenching rains. School was closed; Monsieur Henri and some of the other teachers were in the army. "It's the best thing to come out of this war," Katrin said.

And it gave me time to do the chores. Mémé worked hard, I knew that, but everything was an effort for her, and I scurried around, feeding animals, pulling up cabbages, trying to do what had to be done, even though she was as miserable as ever. The cat still glared at me, and I'd given her a name now, Tiger.

Then it was December. Why had I thought the war would be over before Christmas? *Aunt Marie coming down the attic stairs, balancing boxes of ornaments and garlands to trim the tree. Presents for each other.*

Aunt Marie would be home now, knowing what I'd done.

She wrote a tearstained letter. *You say I told you to do the right thing. What I meant by that was doing your homework and cleaning your bedroom. I am so angry, Geneviève, and terrified for you. I am frantic for your safety, but there's no way I can think of to get you home. Be careful. I love you so much.*

In bed I stared at the crack that ran along the ceiling. Aunt Marie had never been angry with me before. Not once, as long as I could remember. "Homesick," I whispered. It really was a sickness; my eyes burned, my chest was tight. I fell asleep to dream of our tree last year with its ornaments and silver tinsel shining like thin icicles.

And then it was Christmas Eve. That day, a small goose lay in a roasting pan, and a box was at my plate. Mémé turned from the sink. "Open it."

Inside were small wooden figures: a horse with a flowing tail, a cat, a dog like Louis, a reindeer with antlers, and a house that was a miniature of Mémé's. "Jean, the woodcutter, carved them for the tree long ago," she said. "Except for the cat. That was your father's work." She held it up. "He was sixteen."

The cat was a mess, one leg shorter than the other, an ear missing, its wire whiskers bent. I grinned, and even Mémé smiled a little.

In the center of the table was a wooden shoe, almost the size of my foot. "My father made it for me when I was ten," she said. "Leave it at the hearth. Perhaps Père Noël will have something for you." She piled ingredients on the table: nutmeg and ginger, flour, a few eggs, a pitcher of milk, and a tin pan shaped like a boy.

Gingerbread!

Later, from the window, she pointed to a small tree at the edge of the field. "Chop it down," she said.

"You think I could chop down a tree?" I could hear the surprise in my voice, and without thinking, blurted, "You want a Christmas tree?"

"Christmas trees began in Alsace," she said, as if she couldn't believe I didn't know that.

I pressed my lips together and went out to the barn to find an axe. Imagine!

I spent an hour circling the tree, cutting here, chopping there, muttering to Louis the whole time. "Crazy woman thinks I can cut down a tree." But at last, it fell over. "Amazing, Louis. We did it!" I dragged it back to the kitchen with the dog ahead of me, and Tiger, the cat, darting out of the way.

Mémé had managed to put a wooden stand in one corner, and I set the tree up, breathing in the smell of pine.

"Hang the figures," she said as I washed my hands at the pump in the kitchen.

Would I do it alone? But she looped the wooden cat over one branch and the reindeer over another. I dropped the tiny horse under the table and crawled around searching, hearing her sigh.

Later she hobbled from the table to the hearth, putting the goose on to cook, rolling out a tart. And that night, we went to midnight Mass, Mémé leaning on my arm.

Outside the church, one of the farmers drove up in a car. A car! It was the first one I'd seen since I'd arrived in Alsace.

Afterward we ate the goose, the outside crispy, the inside stuffed with mushrooms and chestnuts. We had green beans and then the tart. André would have loved that dinner. I loved it.

Christmas morning came, and the shoe was filled with candies. A gingerbread boy lay on my plate and a present on my chair.

"I have nothing for you," I blurted. "I'm sorry. I didn't think we'd—"

She waved one hand. "I don't need anything."

I tore open the paper. Inside was a sweater she'd knitted, a beautiful blue, almost the color of André's eyes. "It's the best. Really..." I had a quick thought of something Aunt Marie had said once: *Sometimes people surprise you.* Mémé had spent hours knitting the sweater in secret, hours making last night's feast.

Someone was knocking at the door. "I can't imagine...," Mémé said. "Christmas morning."

"Maybe Katrin?"

But Rémy stood there, my battered suitcase in his hand.

"How did you ever find it?" I was sputtering. "How did you know it was mine?"

"I found it in the woods." He grinned, his eyes dancing. "It was open, so I went through it. . . ."

My underwear? My face was hot.

"American clothes." It was almost as if he knew what I was thinking.

I swallowed. "Thank you. I'm so glad to have it."

"Merry Christmas, Gen." He went along the gravel path, waving back at me.

It wasn't until later that I realized the string bag with the books was missing.

Had someone taken them? I wondered.

# eight

School began after the holidays, when I'd hoped to get through the year without it. "Don't worry," Katrin said as we walked; she linked her arm in mine. "It will be fine. You'll see."

I looked at her smiling face, her plump cheeks. She was almost like the sister I'd never had.

And she was right; it was fine. The schoolyard was filled, and in two minutes she'd pulled me over to a couple of girls. "This is Genevieve," she said, "a new friend."

They grinned as Katrin pointed to each one. "Liane plays the piano, even in her head," she said. "Aline is the best at math, and Yvonne is so shy, she barely talks."

I saw Rémy on the other side of the yard and he raised one hand, waving.

Then it was time for classes. Not so different from home! The days went by with homework and chores. Mémé taught me to cook spaetzle, a pasta I'd never tasted before, and spicy bread with dried pears. Snow came and then thawed. I tried to coax friendship from Tiger with tiny morsels of chicken. Then the sun grew warmer. Home seemed forever away. But by the time school ended for the summer, I didn't have to worry about school anymore, and I'd made friends.

I had something else to worry about. Something much worse! In June, Paris fell and France lost the war. What would happen now? But those who had been evacuated from the border began to wander back, and everything seemed the same in the village.

The strawberries were ripe, lettuce grew in rows and asparagus fronds waved in the breeze. Overhead, bees flitted among the peach blossoms. Katrin and I sat on the steps, waving our hands to keep them away.

"Loud, aren't they!" she said, her face to the sun.

Too loud.

"Not bees," I said.

The rumble grew louder. Katrin tilted her head. "What could it be? Motors?"

I clutched her arm as we stared down the road. "Germans!"

She patted my hand. "I'm not afraid."

I turned to the window. Mémé was behind the curtain. "Come inside, Genevieve." She tapped the pane with her thimble. "Come now."

"You too, Katrin," I said.

She shook her head, her curls flying. "I'm going to watch."

"Genevieve," Mémé said urgently.

Motorcycles with sidecars came down the road, sending up clouds of dust, the drivers' faces half-covered by helmets. I edged my way inside and peered out the window with Mémé. A jeep stopped in front, and one of the soldiers motioned to Katrin. My mouth went dry as she walked toward him.

The soldier pointed, and Katrin glanced back at the house. They talked for a moment before he roared away in his jeep. I held the door open for her, but only a few inches.

"What did he say?" I asked.

"He wanted to know who lived here and how many rooms there were. He said he liked the house and he'd be back. Exciting, isn't it!"

Mémé's back was rigid, and I felt a tick in my throat. But gradually the motors died away, and Katrin went out through the field to her house.

Mémé and I sank down at the table. "The soldiers are here to stay," she said. "Officers might want places to sleep."

"Will they put us out? Where would we go?"

"There's that." Was that fear in her voice? "Maybe they'll just take a room or two."

Nazis in the house? Here with us?

In the next few weeks, scores of people came down the road. The Germans were deporting Jewish people and families of men who'd fought against them in the Great War. Some of the people carried children, others staggered along with bundles in their arms or pulled small wagons piled high. They looked hot and tired.

"They weren't even allowed to take their money, or gold, or jewelry, not even their wedding rings," Mémé said bitterly. "They have nothing left. Their homes are gone, all their things."

I pictured myself on that road, walking, not knowing where I was going. I tried not to think of soldiers invading our house.

# *nine*

$\mathcal{S}$umm*er* was almost over. I saw jeeps going by, but the Germans didn't bother us.

"Not yet," Mémé said.

The fields were bursting with vegetables ready to be harvested. I did most of the chores, but Mémé helped as much as she could, her jaws clenched, never complaining.

I'd been here more than a year. A second tearstained letter had gotten through from Aunt Marie. With every word, I could see how frightened she was for me. I kept writing to her, though, hoping my mail would arrive, telling her I was sorry but that I was all right and I'd come home when I could. Most of all, I told her I loved her.

These days I was up earlier than usual, rolling out of bed, my eyes still half-closed, my back and shoulders

aching from all the bending, digging carrots and potatoes from their nests in the soil.

During the day, Louis followed, always with me.
Most of the time I forgot to put him out at night; he
slept on the rag rug next to my bed. If Mémé noticed,
she didn't say anything. Tiger hunted outside and rarely
came into the house.

Mémé and I went from the field to the kitchen, pots
steaming, lids clattering. Up late, we sealed jars with
vegetables and jam and hung garlic on hooks. One
small cellar room held baskets of potatoes; another held
apples.

I fed the animals, edging eggs from under the hens
and keeping my distance from the pig, which was huge
now, ready to be slaughtered, poor thing. But I had to
admit I'd love the sausages, the bacon, the roasts we'd
have this winter.

One morning, Mémé said, "School tomorrow."

I shook my head. "I can't." Burrs knotted my hair,
my nails were cracked, my face and hands so filthy
every day, it was hard to get them clean.

"You must."

I opened my mouth, but before I could say a word,

she began again. "Everyone who lives on a farm manages both."

Both! More cabbages to be taken in, cut into strips and weighed down in brine for sauerkraut. Squash. A last row of potatoes. And long days of school with homework every night.

"All right," I muttered, seeing her stubborn face.

I spent that night pouring bleach over my hands, scrubbing my face until it was raw and washing my hair under the pump.

The next day, Katrin came up the path, books in her arms.

Behind her, a truck stopped in front. One of the soldiers slammed out, and we hesitated, to go past him.

He came toward us. "Someone said you have a pig ready to be slaughtered," he said.

I didn't answer.

He motioned to two others and they walked up the path. "We're here for the pig," he said.

"Please." I was almost whispering. "We have to eat."

"So does the German army," he said.

I saw Mémé at the window, shaking her head at me, so Katrin and I went back into the kitchen while the men dragged the pig away.

"How did they know? Who told them?" I asked.

Mémé's face was stony. "We always have a pig. Everyone knows that."

"Yes, everyone," Katrin said. "We lost our pig to them yesterday. And the cow too." She leaned forward, whispering. "We're hiding food now, as much as we can. I think everyone will be doing that."

On the way to school, I couldn't stop thinking of the pig and the meat that wouldn't be ours this winter. I thought about how all of us would manage to hide food.

We reached the square and stopped. The Germans had toppled a stone statue of a French soldier from the Great War. A cloud of gray rose from the base, and small chunks were scattered underneath.

I wondered if we'd be late, but it didn't matter. Everyone was still outside the school, gathered around a paper taped to the wall: it was a long list with a huge black VERBOTEN printed across the top. *Forbidden.*

We couldn't speak French anymore. Our names and street names would be changed to German. Wedding rings had to be worn on the right hand in the German way.

Katrin twitched her shoulder. "Not important."

I stared at her.

"Many people here speak German all the time, especially those who were alive when Alsace belonged to Germany. Now we'll all think German, speak German. We'll have to be German."

She pointed to the list with one finger. "Listen to this. Radios have to be turned in to the village hall. And something else . . ."

I leaned forward. On the bottom of the list I read: *All books not written in German must be burned immediately!*

Where were my books, one in French, the others in English, and my name in all of them? Who had them now?

All I could think of was that list and what it meant. I wouldn't be able to keep my French name, and André had told me that Mémé had never taken her wedding ring off. Now she'd have to change it to her other hand.

Inside after art class, the principal came in, with a man following. The principal spoke in German: "Welcome your new history teacher, Herr Albert."

"Where's Monsieur Henri?" someone asked. It was what all of us were wondering.

There was no expression on the principal's face. "He is no longer with us."

The new teacher spoke up. "In prison, of course. He was a soldier, after all."

The new teacher's sleeves didn't cover his wrists. His pants were baggy. He snapped his feet together, then raised his arm in the Hitler salute. "*Guten Morgen.*"

"*Guten Morgen,*" we parroted back, and sank into our seats as the principal went out the door.

Herr Albert asked our names, pointing from desk to desk. Immediately after the last student spoke, he repeated them, all of them correct. Herr Albert might look sloppy, but his brain was sharp. He wasn't finished, though; he changed some of our names on the spot. Yvonne became Helga; I became Gerta.

He glanced at the tricolor flag hanging in front. With one motion he pulled it down and dropped it into the wastebasket. "No need for this anymore." He ignored the gasps that came from the back of the room.

He reached into his valise and took out the Nazi flag with its swastika like a black spider. He unfolded it and, reaching up, threaded it into the holder.

Liane looked down at her desk and moved her fingers, playing an imaginary piano. Claude looked furious, and my chest felt tight, almost as if someone were squeezing me too hard.

Herr Albert rubbed his hands together. "We'll begin our study of history now." He pointed to the wall map. "Alsace is a strip of land between the Vosges Mountains and the Rhine River," he said, as if every five-year-old in Alsace didn't know that. "It was German from 1871 to the end of the First World War. Then, sadly, it became French."

By this time he'd lost us. Katrin and I passed notes back and forth, choosing crazy names for everyone in the class. I jumped as I realized Herr Albert was standing in front of me. "There's no time for gossip in my room." He leaned closer. "In the seventeen hundreds you would have to walk through the village wearing the Klapperstein."

What was he talking about? Katrin looked as confused as I was. But he went on. "A huge stone. Gossips wore it around their necks, weighing them down."

Laughter bubbled up as I thought of our wearing it, inching our way through the village. Katrin bit her lip, trying to look serious.

Herr Albert's face changed. No longer did he look like a messy teacher, but more like someone to fear. "We are German now," he said. "And you will see change all over Europe."

I swallowed and looked down at my desk as he crumpled Katrin's note. If only this terrible day would end.

# ten

*The* next Saturday, I came into the kitchen carrying cabbages, almost like babies, from the wheelbarrow.

Mémé locked the door behind me. "We have things to do."

I nibbled at a square of cheese from the table as she dropped a rubber mat in front of the armoire. "You might as well know about this," she said. "I'll let you help me."

She was impossible, I told myself for the hundredth time. I pushed back my chair and stood up as she straightened the mat with one foot. "We must move the armoire, and the stone floor can't be marked."

What was she talking about? How could we move that huge cabinet? How could I do it? She had no strength left.

"I moved this in the Great War with Gérard," she said. "Push, Genevieve."

Inch by inch, I managed to open a space behind the armoire, wide enough to squeeze through. I stared into that dusty space, almost the size of the pantry.

"But why . . . ," I began.

"A place to store food, to keep us alive. Do you think I'd let the Germans come in here and take everything?"

I raised my hand to my throat.

She handed me a rag and I slid inside to wipe down the shelves. We went from pantry to armoire, filling them.

"Take only half. We have to eat, after all."

Almost finished, I kept looking at the shelves. The vegetables inside the glass jars were almost like jewels, the green beans, the golden pears, the red peppers. I tripped and the last jar of tomatoes slipped out of my hands. Mémé wasn't paying attention, though. It was as if she hadn't heard the glass smashing, or seen the red swath spreading around the broken jar. She pinched my sleeve. "We can't trust anyone. Tell no one, Genevieve."

I thought of the people I'd met here: Rémy, Madame Jacques at the bakery, her son, Claude, even

Monsieur Philippe, the bookseller, with his thick lips and unfriendly face.

Katrin and I talked about everything: how much money the bistro owner had hidden under his mattress, how many tarts Madame Jacques ate every day, how many hours Liane played the piano.

And Mémé. Of course, Mémé.

I knelt to pick up the shards of glass.

"You'll see," Mémé said. "There are those who are French, and others who are German sympathizers."

I nodded uncertainly.

"Promise me. Give me your word."

"All right." I crossed my fingers. I didn't bother to look at her. Surely it was all right to tell Katrin.

Slowly I pushed the armoire back into place, thinking of my father doing this so many years ago.

There was only the half-filled pantry to tell us what we'd done.

# *eleven*

*In* November, a mild wind swept over the field. "A good day to air the quilts," Mémé said.

I came around the side of the house with a quilt to hang, and stopped. An officer stood there, medals weighing down his uniform. A soldier stood behind him, his face covered with freckles; he must have been André's age.

I hugged the quilt to me. Where was Mémé?

The officer pointed, his boot resting on the bottom rail of the fence. "There's a horse in the field."

I glanced toward Sister.

He smiled with perfect teeth. "As long as we're all Germans, we have to share everything. What's the horse's name?"

"Sister. No one rides her. We just harness her up to the cart . . ."

A mistake. I knew it right away, and maybe the young soldier did too. He bent his head.

"Ah." The officer laughed. "I'll just borrow them both."

"Please," I began, but I couldn't stop him.

He climbed the fence, whistling for Sister. She came immediately, hoping for a sugar cube or an apple slice, and he opened the gate for her. He snapped his fingers at the young soldier. "Get the cart from the barn. Harness her."

The young soldier's face was red, his freckles standing out. Did he feel sorry for me?

Moments later, Sister and the cart were gone, rattling up the road toward the village. I felt tears of grief. What would André have done? Worse, what would Mémé say? I flew upstairs. She was in her bedroom, a mop in her hand. "Oh, Mémé, he took the horse."

She looked up. "What are you talking about?"

"And the cart. An officer."

The mop slid away from her. "My horse?"

Would she yell at me? Cry the way I was crying? Instead she clenched her hands into fists. "An old horse." She raised her head. "A rickety cart."

"Why are you saying that? She's a wonderful horse, and without the cart we can't go far."

"There's nothing we can do," Mémé said.

"Could we complain to someone?"

"Better to keep still. We don't want to be noticed."

It was too late; we had been noticed. Toward the end of the day, another German came, riding a motorcycle. He left it in front and strolled around to the back of the house, his boots heavy on the gravel.

Mémé was still in her bedroom. I called her from the stairs. "A German is outside."

"I'll be right there," she said.

She came down a few minutes later, but she didn't wait for him to knock. "Can I help you?" she said as she opened the door.

"You have a big house, with only the two of you?"

She barely nodded.

How did he know that? And then I realized. He must have been the German who'd spoken to Katrin!

"You have extra rooms, then," he said. "Perhaps . . ."

He went past her, through the kitchen into the hall. "The stairs?"

"There's a room down here," Mémé said, the German words sounding strange on her tongue.

"I wouldn't want to disturb you. Let's see what's on the second floor."

What could we do? We followed him upstairs, Mémé walking slowly as she'd done all year. We watched as he opened doors and stopped at her room, his hand on the molding.

The painting was gone. A pale square against darker paint stood out on the wall. He noticed it too. He walked in, circled the bed and stared, his hands clenched behind his back.

Mémé started back down the hall toward the stairs.

"*Frau*," he called after her, his voice sharp.

She turned, waiting. Louis padded up the stairs and stood close to her. Even the dog knew something was wrong. Mémé put her hand on his head.

"Is the dog vicious?" the soldier asked.

"Certainly not."

"Yes. We wouldn't want to get rid of him."

My heart was pounding. First Sister. Now Louis?

"What hung on the wall?" The German ran one finger over the pale square.

She didn't hesitate. "A mirror. Shattered."

He glanced at me, and my eyes slid away from him; I

stared down at the floor. Was that the edge of the frame just under the bed?

He stood at the dresser now, running his fingers over Mémé's necklace. "This room will do nicely. I'll bring my things this afternoon."

We couldn't look at him. He'd just changed our lives.

"Perhaps I'll see the shards from the mirror later," he said as he went downstairs. "But in the meantime, hang something pleasant to look at."

Mémé leaned against the wall, and I bent to bury my cheek in Louis's fur. "It's under the bed," I whispered.

"Yes. But first, we want to be sure he's gone. He can guess the painting is valuable."

I went down to the hall window, and she was right. The motorcycle was still there. I edged my way along the hall, peering into the kitchen.

He was standing at the massive sink. I backed away and up the stairs. Moments later, I heard the roar of the motorcycle. "He's gone."

"We'll use the space overhead," Mémé said. "It was meant for workers a hundred years ago. A pull-down stair went up from your bedroom, but Gérard plastered it over during the Great War, so there's only one way to get there."

She slid the painting from under the bed and wrapped it in a pillowcase. "You'll have to go out on the roof from your bedroom, Genevieve."

How could I do that? The drop was terrifying. She stared at me, almost daring me to say I couldn't do it. I knew what would happen. She'd try it herself, never mind the ankle that still gave her trouble. There she'd be, a bag of bones rolling down the slanted roof and hitting the gravel far below.

We went into my room, and I opened my window, staring out, trying not to look down.

"Climb onto the sill," Mémé said.

It was much wider than the one at home. I put one knee up, then the other, crouching, moving outside, my hands glued to the bottom of the frame.

"Reach up, Genevieve. You'll feel the ledge at the top of the window."

I leaned back, one hand still clutching the frame, the other reaching . . .

And grasped it. It took forever to make myself stand on the top of the ledge, three stories above the ground.

The wind pulled at my dress and hair; behind me came the steady tap-tapping of loose tiles.

I touched the window above and, stretching, managed to shove it open, my heart fluttering.

"Good." Mémé held the painting up to me, the pillowcase flapping.

Then, the rumble of a motor. Was the officer back? He couldn't have gone far.

I pushed the painting inside and saw him at the end of the gravel path. I scrambled into a small room, the dust thick on the floor, cobwebs like fine net stretched across the corners. I huddled there, shaking, the painting in my arms. Vaguely, I heard Mémé shut the bedroom window below.

After a while, I rested the painting against the wall, careful to avoid jutting nails. On the floor was a thin straw mattress, and I crouched down on it, trembling. "All right," I whispered, "I'm all right."

I ran my hand over the dusty floor at my side, feeling grit under my nails. And then I felt something else. Deep cuts had been carved into the wood, almost the size of my fists. I ran my fingers over them, realizing they were letters, *G.M.*

My father's initials, for his name, Gérard Michel. My initials too.

Without thinking, I patted the carving almost as if I might be patting Louis's broad head. For the first time, I didn't visualize a grim-faced man with a beard. I saw someone my age, kneeling there, carving.

The initials had been here all this time, almost as if they were waiting to find me.

And something else. As the sun began to set, it threw light on the opposite wall so I could see stick figures of two girls wearing enormous bows, and the face of a boy with a huge smiling mouth.

My father? A boy. Not the funny drawing of a grumpy man. I felt warmth spread through my chest. But I went back to thinking of the German soldier invading our farmhouse. Wouldn't he want to know where I was?

# twelve

Wrapping my arms around my waist, I tried to keep warm. I kept sneezing from layers of dust, but I must have slept.

I dreamed of a house, roses growing in front. Our own house in Springfield Gardens. Home.

I awoke to the sound of wind, stronger now. Outside, there was almost no light. I stood up, but I couldn't see if the motorcycle was still on the path.

Was the officer in the house? I'd take a chance and slide down the roof, leaving the painting safe against the wall.

I could do it.

I climbed out backward, leaning hard against the sloping roof. I found my window ledge with one foot, crouched and grabbed it with both hands, my feet sliding down to the stone sill.

Mémé was there. She steadied my legs, then held my waist, guiding me into the bedroom. "I told him you were resting, that you had a headache," she whispered. "We'll go along the hall quietly, past my room, where he stares at a terrible painting I've placed on the wall, and soils my quilt with his boots. We'll tiptoe downstairs and fortify ourselves for whatever we'll have to deal with."

What we dealt with first was arranging the extra bedroom beyond the kitchen for us both, pulling quilts and pillows out of the chest. We'd leave upstairs for him.

At the kitchen table, I made myself eat. I was worn out, and so glad André was safe at college in New York.

"One more thing." Mémé spoke as if the words were being forced out of her. "Louis must go."

"Please, no." He was under the table, his muzzle on my instep. "He'll be quiet. He's such a good dog, so gentle."

She peered up at the ceiling as if she could see the German officer on the second floor. "The dog needs to be safe." She hesitated. "I would take him, but I don't want you alone here with the German."

"Louis loves us."

She raised one hand to stop my words. "You'll go through the field, over the wall, and find Jean, the woodcutter. He's a kind man. He'll keep Louis close so he can't come back to us. Maybe someday . . ."

I was crying again. Everyone I loved was disappearing, everyone was flying away.

I went to the door, and Louis followed me outside, almost as if he understood what was happening.

Tonight there was only a sliver of moon. I hesitated until my eyes became used to the shape of the field and the forest beyond. We walked slowly, Louis leading me now, until we crossed the low stone wall.

I stopped, hearing voices. I reached for Louis's collar, but my fingers slid along his back and he kept going.

"It's the Michels' dog," someone said.

I knew the voice.

The woodcutter answered, "Yes, his name is Louis."

I went forward to see Rémy crouched on the ground, petting the dog. The woodcutter turned as he heard me.

"My grandmother asked if you would take Louis for us," I said.

"A good dog. But why?"

"A German officer is going to stay at the house. He doesn't like dogs, and we're afraid . . ." I couldn't finish.

Rémy looked up at me, his eyes burning. "What kind of a man dislikes dogs?"

The woodcutter put his broad hand on my shoulder. "Tell Elise . . . . Tell your grandmother . . ." He shook his head. "She'll know." He reached for Louis's collar.

"I'll bring back food for him," I said.

He waved his hand. "No need, I'll take care of him." Then it was almost as if he and the dog melted into the trees, in front of me one moment, gone the next.

"I'm sorry, Gen," Rémy said. "Really sorry you're not back in your New York." He smiled. "But think how lucky you are to be at your grandmother's beautiful farm."

I had to smile too. I lifted one hand, then went across the wall to Mémé, wondering what Rémy was doing there.


A few days later I was on my way to meet Katrin for school when the German officer cornered me at the end of the path. "Where's the dog, *Fraülein*?"

I stared at the ground. Mémé and I should have decided what to say to him, but we'd never thought he'd be interested enough to ask.

Digging my toe into the gravel, I tried to think. "He ran away."

"An old dog like that?"

"He does that sometimes."

"Then he'll be back."

"I don't know."

But he'd lost interest in Louis and me. He straddled his motorcycle and sped away.

Katrin waited for me at her gate, ready to talk, but I raised my hand, saying, "Wait," while I thought about how I'd tell her what had happened.

We kept going, but finally I held up my hand again. "Listen." I was almost whispering.

Katrin turned, her head close to mine. "What is it?"

By the time we saw the school, I'd told her everything I could think of: the attic room, the painting, Louis.

I wondered what Mémé would say if she knew. But she wouldn't know. Katrin would keep our secret, I was sure of it.

# RESISTANCE

# thirteen

$\mathcal{J}t$ was hard to concentrate in school. My thoughts wandered to the German officer, who would be looking over our shoulders all the time now, to Louis, who used to pad up to my bedroom at night. I made myself think of happier things: my father's carving, Rémy's smile. I grinned to myself, picturing Tiger, the three-colored cat who reminded me a little of Mémé with her suspicious eyes, her unfriendly face.

At last, it was time to go home. Katrin and I reached the square and saw soldiers in front of the bookshop. Monsieur Philippe came outside with a pile of books in his arms. He dropped them in the street and went back for more.

"French books," Katrin whispered.

Soldiers drenched them with a can of something—turpentine, maybe—and threw a match onto the pile. Philippe stood there talking with them as flames shot up, devouring the books. He kicked one farther into the fire; the pages curled up, lighted and were gone. Didn't he care?

One of the soldiers elbowed him, laughing, and Philippe said, "Enough of the French, eh?"

I couldn't watch anymore. "Let's go," I told Katrin.

At the end of the square, I glanced down the alley to see Rémy with a piece of chalk in his hand. He drew lines on the stone, then disappeared toward the back of the pharmacy. "What was he doing?"

"Drawing the Cross of Lorraine."

"But what does it mean?"

"It's a symbol from the medieval days. Free France!" She frowned. "If you look, you'll see it everywhere. The Germans can't bear it. They're making people wash it off, or paint over it. And if they ever catch anyone doing it, there'll be trouble, arrests and maybe worse."

Why had Rémy taken such a chance?

We walked the rest of the way, both of us quiet. I left her at her gate and crossed the wall. There was just enough ink in my pen to draw the cross on one of the stones.

*Free France.*

Mémé was in the kitchen, her left finger bandaged,

covering her ring. She must have heard about the new rules. "I won't take it off," she said fiercely.

I slid into the chair across from her.

"The Germans came today. They've taken the cow." She spread her hands wide. "The hens too."

I felt the tears that had been threatening all day.

"They've left almost nothing," she said.

"The bicycles?"

"Still there."

"They were too old, too rusty, I guess."

Mémé stood, leaning on the table for a moment, then went to the counter. "Vegetable soup. At least we'll have that. And the potatoes and apples are still in the cellar rooms."

The German came in then, without knocking. "Soup? I'll trouble you for some too."

How would we ever retrieve the food behind the armoire? The German, whose name we knew now was Fürst, appeared when we least expected him. We watched at the windows for him; still, he managed to surprise us. We had to be careful of everything we did, everything we said.

That evening, Mémé and I went to our room early. We locked the door and pulled the radio out from its hiding place under a pile of quilts, turning it on just loud enough to catch the solemn voice of the newscaster. The news had been terrible all year: so many countries had fallen to the Germans.

Before we had time to listen, a sudden boom rattled the windowpanes. In one motion, Mémé pulled back the quilt and I flew to the window, Mémé right behind me. Beyond the village was a glow of orange, almost as if the sun had risen.

Fürst's boots clumped down the stairs and stopped. Mémé threw the quilt over the radio, but he kept going through the hall and into the kitchen. The outside door slammed, and the motorcycle roared as he sped toward the village.

"What is it?" I asked, but Mémé shook her head.

We watched the glow soften and eventually disappear. We went back to bed, but not to sleep until the night was almost over.

"What do you think happened?" I asked Katrin the next morning.

"My brother, Karl, told me. They blew up the railway station and ruined as much of the tracks as they could."

I thought of the station, the pigeons flying overhead,

the crêpes dotted with sugar. "Why would the Germans do that?"

She raised her eyebrows. "Are you five years old? It was the French, trying to stop the Germans from deporting people, from drafting Alsatian men to fight for them. The Resistance!"

It was the first time I'd heard that word.

We stopped at the square. Even this far from the station, smoke hung in the air with a strong smell of burning, almost like licorice. Soldiers rushed back and forth.

Outside the school, we waited for the principal to call us inside, hearing the word *Resistance* again and again, and another word, *sabotage*.

In our history class, Herr Albert called the roll, staring at each one of us as he said our names. "If anyone knows about the fire, he must tell, otherwise he will be as guilty as the saboteurs."

My heart thumped. He made me feel as if I were in danger, even though I didn't know anything about it. I was glad to escape from his room and go to the science laboratory, where the teacher filled bottles with different-colored water that seemed to be useless.

That afternoon, Mémé sat in the rocker knitting

socks. "Rémy's father has been arrested," she said. "He's been taken to Shirmeck prison. Clara Moeller stopped by to tell me."

I could hardly breathe. "What about Rémy's mother and his little sister, Cécile?"

"They were lucky. A courier will take them to Switzerland."

I could hardly get the word out. "Rémy?"

"Missing. If they find him ..."

I thought of the Cross of Lorraine, and Rémy at the woodcutter's the other day. Was he there now?

The door opened and Fürst came in. "It's snowing," he said in a pleasant voice.

Mémé turned away from him, and I pretended I didn't see him go toward the coal stove and bend over it. I knew it was cold and empty.

"You'll have to use more fuel, Frau Meyer," he said, using our new German name. "Don't hoard it. We'll all be sick from the drafts."

Mémé's back stiffened.

He saw my eyes. He must have known I hated him. There wasn't enough coal to last the winter. But what did he care? He wanted to be warm now. And later?

Maybe he'd find somewhere else to stay. I could only hope that.

He went up to the bedroom, and Mémé laid her knitting on the table. "I wouldn't ask this . . ."

"You don't have to ask. I'm going to the woodcutter's to look for Rémy."

"Go now. Go carefully, though. It's cold and windy."

I wrapped my coat and one of her old scarves around me and left the house without a sound. Outside, the snow was beginning to cover the ground. I ran, slipping and sliding across the field. I didn't see the low stone wall and went headlong across it. The fall took my breath, and my knees burned, beginning to bleed.

I could almost hear Mémé's voice. "I told you."

I scrambled up. The wind was biting my face, closing my eyes so the world was hidden and everything was disappearing. I peered ahead. How could I find my way to the woodcutter's small house buried in the trees?

# fourteen

*The* woodcutter came forward, his footsteps silent. Louis bounded toward me, his fur covered with snow, his tail waving. I leaned against him, running my hand over his head and his back. So much had happened since he'd slept at the foot of my bed.

I took a chance. "Is Rémy with you?" I whispered. "Is he all right?" If only I could see him smiling at me, or touching my shoulder.

The woodcutter bent his head close to mine. "He can't stay here safely for long." He took a breath. "His arm was burned enough to worry about infection. The Germans will be watching for that. He'll have to disappear." He shook his head. "The poor boy: his father gone, his mother and sister taking that dangerous trip to Switzerland. Even the pharmacy has been shuttered. All the medicines belong to the Germans now."

Oh, Rémy. But I knew what we had to do. Somehow we'd bring him to the house, help him across the roof and into that small attic room. "We'll take him as soon as the German sleeps," I said.

No matter what, I'd see Rémy again!

The woodcutter held Louis's collar, and I turned to stumble back over the low stone wall and crossed the field.

The German officer stood in the kitchen, leaning against the table, his coat over his shoulders. "Where have you been?"

"I told you—" Mémé began, but he raised his hand. "Let the girl tell me herself."

What had she told him? What could I say?

I barely said anything. "The snow, lovely—" I began, and broke off. "I'm going to be sick." Hand to my mouth, I rushed past him, down the hall, and closed the bedroom door.

It was the best I could do.

Moments later, Mémé came into the room. "You never cease to surprise me, Genevieve."

I didn't tell her that I'd fallen and scraped my knees against the wall. I thought of that stone with its Cross of Lorraine, and no way to erase it. She'd say, "You don't think!"

I sat on the bed and, lips hardly moving, told her what the woodcutter had said.

She stared at the window, nodding.

I went to the half-opened bedroom door and stood, listening, until we were sure Fürst slept. The wait was endless.

"Something else to think about. We need a signal." Mémé worried her forehead with her bandaged finger. "Your father's carved cat!"

I remembered! One leg shorter than the other, wire whiskers. Christmas was coming in just a few days. Another Christmas!

"If it's safe, I'll hang the cat in the window," she said.

I nodded. I'd look for it.

It was almost midnight when I went back across the field; the snow had stopped and a misty moon gleamed overhead. The woodcutter was there waiting to lead me to his house.

Rémy lay on a cot, his eyes closed. He started up as he heard me whisper his name. "Gen!" He tried to smile, and I touched his hand, so glad to see him, but frightened about the terrible danger we were all in.

"Play with fire," he began the old saying, "you're going to get burned."

I swallowed. "I'm sorry," I said. "Really . . ."

"My father was betrayed," he said. "But who was it?"

There was anger in the woodcutter's voice. "We can't be sure of anyone."

Almost Mémé's exact words.

We left quickly, the woodcutter holding Louis's collar and talking gently to the crying dog.

Crossing the field, I watched our window. The cat wasn't there. I saw movement: Fürst, walking around the table.

I put my arms around Rémy to steady him and we sank down in the wet snow to wait. It was almost dawn, both of us shivering, when Fürst banged out of the house. I saw him kick at Tiger, who snarled and raced around the side of the house. Then Fürst straddled his motorcycle and left.

I despised him.

Mémé was at the window, hanging the cat; its wire whiskers caught the light. Her hand was raised, beckoning.

"Now," I told Rémy. We stumbled to our feet and walked across the rest of the field. Inside, Mémé slid a jar of water into my pocket for him. "A small bathroom behind the eaves," she whispered.

We took the stairs, one slow step at a time to my bedroom.

Flakes of snow swirled on the sill as I raised the window. "We have to go out there," I said. "It won't be easy."

"It's all right," he whispered.

We climbed the slippery roof together. It was much harder than the first time I'd done it. But at last, we were in that dusty room.

Rémy slid down on the straw mattress. "Thank you, Gen." His eyes closed, and he was asleep. I watched him, his fine eyelashes, his eyes moving slightly below the lids. He mumbled something—was it *planting*?

I remembered he wanted to be a farmer, to have his own field, like the one we'd seen that summer day.

How tired I was! The night was over and I hadn't slept. I couldn't wait to go downstairs and throw myself into bed.

But first, I worked off his boots and threw my coat over him, seeing that the burn on his arm was covered with torn rags.

I bent to touch my father's initials, thinking how strange it was that they comforted me. I ran my hand over the pillowcase that held the painting; it was streaked with dust. The painting shouldn't have been here.

So many things that shouldn't have been.

I climbed down to Mémé, my knees stiff, wishing I could put the painting back where it belonged.

Wishing!

My head was filled with wishes.

# fifteen

*Was* Fürst back? I heard the sound of a motorcycle, but then it faded away.

Mémé followed me inside the bedroom, carrying a cup of broth, hot and steaming. "Don't sleep," she whispered as if he were standing in the hall.

I could hardly keep my eyes open. The wind outside was strong, the snow blowing across the field. "I have to sleep." I sank down on the edge of the bed.

"You will manage." She barely moved her lips, almost as if Fürst could hear from upstairs. "You will go to school as if everything is normal." She reached out, holding the broth to my lips.

I sipped at it. I could feel myself waking.

"Where is your coat, Genevieve?"

I pointed up.

"Never mind. You can wear mine."

"That would look normal?" In spite of myself, I grinned at her, and I thought I saw her smile. "And what about Rémy? It's so cold, so terrible up there."

"We just have to do the best we can." She went on, her head close to mine. "After school, find a way to delay."

I glanced at her determined face.

"Look at me, Genevieve. You can't let Katrin know about this."

I took a large swallow of broth, so hot it burned my tongue. "Katrin would help, I know she would."

"You don't know."

"All right."

"So. You'll go to Philippe. Tell him you have books but you want something new. He'll know we're sheltering someone, that we need help."

"I can't tell Katrin." I was filled with anger. "But you're willing to let that man know? He burns books without any feelings; he talks to the Germans."

"Genevieve, for once will you listen!"

I didn't answer. We went into the kitchen and I jammed my hat over my head, pulled on her coat and threw a woolen scarf over my shoulders. "All right," I said. There was no help for it. She'd won again.

I spent the day at school, looking out at small cyclones of snow in the air, trying to stay awake. In history, Herr Albert tapped his desk with a pointer. "What is outside, Fraülein Meyer, is not as important as the history I'm teaching."

History! Herr Albert was fascinated by history.

At last school was over. Katrin and I left, our mouths covered with scarves. I hesitated. "Forgot my book." My voice was muffled.

She glanced back toward the school, squinting against the blowing snow. "I'll come with you."

"No, it's too cold."

She nodded. I could see she was grateful as she kept going. When she was just a shadow far ahead, I glanced over my shoulder to be sure I was alone. Then I trudged toward the square.

# sixteen

Soldiers were billeted in the village hall now, and some of them marched along the street in pairs. An old woman had to step off the sidewalk to let them pass. I looked toward the shuttered pharmacy, thinking that the medicine Rémy needed was inside that door, but taken now by the Germans.

In front of me was a house with a pointed roof and wilted flowers in the snow-covered window boxes. I remembered it belonged to a doctor.

Suppose I went in and said my grandmother had burned herself cooking, her fingers grasping the pot handle? Why not? He could give me something to help heal that burn.

I went up the path, and saw the door was open.

No one was inside the waiting room, with its chairs in a row like a theater. I stared at the closed door in front of me, beginning to wonder if I'd done the right thing. Overhead a clock clicked, five minutes, ten. I rapped on the door.

"Yes? Open," the voice said in German from inside.

I stood in the doorway, nervous. The doctor was rail-thin and didn't seem friendly. I wasn't his patient, after all. I tried to act as if nothing much had happened, that only a small burn from the stove had brought me here. "My grandmother needs something for a burn."

"I can't help you."

"You're a doctor."

"Think of what you're saying. The Germans have been here three times asking just that question: who in this village needs something for a burn?"

I took a breath. I understood. "But just a small—"

He wouldn't let me finish. "If they see you coming from here and find that you're carrying a jar of burn medicine, you'll be in prison, and so will I."

I backed out of the room and closed the door behind me.

It was almost dark now. Tendrils of smoke still rose in the distance from the railway station. I crossed the square, passing the butcher's shop, with empty hooks where once huge slabs of meat had hung and the boulangerie, closed now, without bread. The pâtisserie came next, with its shelves almost bare. But Madame Jacques had hung a wreath in the window. I'd almost forgotten: Christmas was in a few days. Christmas again!

I heard the loud singing of soldiers coming from the bistro. I veered past, and then I was in front of the bookshop, peering inside. Dim light came from the storage room in back. I could hardly see the books on the shelves. I trudged around to the alley.

The bookshop's small window was halfway down the alley. The back room wasn't nearly as neat as the front. The walls were unpainted, the clock had stopped at two-thirty, probably years ago, and books were stacked in an uneven pile on a table.

Philippe wasn't there. I glanced at the stairs leading up to his apartment and rapped harder. I had to get home to Rémy.

Philippe came downstairs, a napkin looped around his thick neck, looking annoyed at being disturbed.

I kept knocking. *Hurry. Hurry.*

He moved his huge girth slowly, then opened the door. By this time I'd forgotten Mémé's exact words, so I raised my shoulders. "I want a book," I whispered.

He shook his head.

"We have books—" I began.

He took a quick look down the alley, pulled me inside and pushed me onto a chair. "Never talk when you're outside." His voice was fierce.

I was almost more afraid of him than of the Germans.

"I'm Genevieve Michel," I said.

"I know who you are."

"We have books. But I want another one." My mouth trembled; in spite of myself, I was crying.

"You're too old for tears."

"Rémy . . . ," I began.

He frowned, lines creasing his wide forehead, and raised one hand.

"We have him in the attic. His arm was burned—" I bit off the words.

Philippe stared, silent.

"The doctor wouldn't give me anything for the burn."

He made a sound with his tongue. His face was filled with fury. "Doctor? You went to the doctor?"

I backed away from him. It was a mistake coming here, maybe as much as going to the doctor's. I reached for the doorknob; I'd done what I could.

Philippe held up his hand. "Can you manage for a few days?"

I wanted to say *We can manage forever.* I wanted to say *We don't need you.* But I thought of that room, cold and dark, and we did need him, or someone, to help.

He waited for me to answer. I nodded, then turned the knob and opened the door.

"Tell your grandmother I'll arrange things."

I took a last look at the back of the store and left.

Left too quickly, because I'd seen something on one of the chairs at his table. Bunched-up like a charcoal cat was a wool sweater.

I told myself we were all cold these days without enough coal to warm our stoves. But I knew! The last time I'd seen it, André was wearing that sweater.

My thoughts raced. Could Philippe have given André over to the Germans? But wasn't André safe at home in New York? Wasn't he? I shook my head, turned and went back to the bookshop. I peered in, but from where I was standing, I couldn't see the chair with the sweater. Philippe stood there, staring at a cabinet.

I rapped on the window, and he came to the door again. "What is it?" he asked, almost as if he might be saying *What now, pest?*

"The sweater."

He raised his massive shoulders.

"On the chair." I glanced toward it: a pile of books teetered there now.

"Underneath." I went toward the chair and swept my hand over the books, which toppled onto the floor. There was no sweater; the chair was empty.

I frowned up at him. "I know what I saw."

"Go home."

If only I could. "Where's my brother?"

"Hasn't he been gone since before the war?"

"What did you do with his sweater?"

Philippe shook his head, opened his mouth to say something.

"I saw it. Just now." I was trembling, angry.

"You could be dangerous," he said. "My advice is for you to avoid seeing things." He gripped my shoulder, pushed me to the door and outside; the lock snapped behind me. I pictured André, the sweater looped around his shoulders. André laughing, happy with himself, happy with me.

I slipped down the alley again, past the noisy bistro, then hurried along the empty road back to the farm.

Mémé trusted this man. It was wrong. I felt it. I was sure of it.

Where was André? Could he be here somewhere? Taken by the Germans? Had Philippe betrayed him?

But suppose it wasn't André's sweater?

No. I'd seen the pulls in the sleeve, the zipper not quite matching the color of the wool. Aunt Marie had knitted it. It couldn't have been anyone else's. How did Philippe get it?

At the farm, the motorcycle was gone. Tiger slept on the stone step. I stepped around her and, heartsick, told Mémé that I'd tried to get medicine for Rémy. "The doctor wouldn't give it to me."

She looked at me, horrified. "You asked—" She broke off. "What is the matter with you?"

She was right. I didn't think. I lost things, forgot them, and now the doctor!

But what about Monsieur Philippe? I leaned forward. "I think he sides with the Germans. We can't trust him."

She shook her head.

"But you said to trust no one."

She waved her hand. "Don't talk foolishness to me about Philippe."

I didn't say another word. But I needed someone to talk to, someone I could trust.

Katrin.

I was determined to do what I'd promised not to do. I'd tell her everything she hadn't heard so far.

Yes, in the morning, on the way to school. It was the last day before school closed for the Christmas holidays.

# seventeen

*The* window rattled; someone pulled hard on my arm. I pulled the quilt up higher; I felt as if I'd just fallen asleep.

Mémé? What was she saying?

I opened my eyes and glanced toward the window. Icicles glowed silver in the dark, and sleet peppered the glass.

"Wake up, Genevieve," Mémé said urgently. "The boy is in that freezing room. He needs food and warmer clothing."

Suddenly wide awake, I threw on my clothes, and Mémé handed me two thick sweaters. "Gérard's," she said.

I pulled them on, one over the other; it was almost as if I could feel my father by wearing them. Mémé shoved a chunk of cheese, a wizened apple and a small potato that had been cooked and cooled into one huge pocket, and a jar of water into the other.

She stood at the bottom of the stairs, back rigid. "I would do this," she began, "if only . . ."

I touched her thin shoulder, then tiptoed upstairs. I heard a sound and turned. Fürst stood in the doorway across the hall. "It's the middle of the night, Gerta."

My heart hammered. Sleepwalking? He'd never believe it. "C-cold," I stammered. "I left my robe . . ." My voice trailed off.

"Even with those sweaters." He shook his head. "She doesn't give us enough heat," he said, and disappeared inside.

I went into my old bedroom, locked the door behind me and sat on the edge of the bed, shaking. Outside, the roof tiles were slick with ice. Could I open the window without a sound?

But Rémy was crouched up there with wind and cold coming in through the chinks around the window, without anything to eat. I had to do this.

It took forever to raise the icy window. Head down, I

went out; the roof tiles chattered in the wind. I climbed, the sleet stinging, forcing me to close my eyes. I reached up and held on to the sill, fingers tapping on the attic window.

*Open, Rémy. Open.*

He leaned out to me, his hands colder than mine.

I slid onto the floor, unable to talk, hardly able to move. He put one arm out, hugging me. *Ah, Rémy.*

"Wait." I shrugged off both sweaters. "Put them on."

He shook his head. "You'll freeze."

"Put them on right away." I sounded like Mémé.

He grinned and reached for them, wincing as he pulled a sleeve over his arm.

"Sorry," I said, wincing with him.

He shrugged. "I was too close when the explosion went off. But it was worth it, every bit of it, and it won't be the end. The Resistance fighters won't stop until the Germans are sent back across the Rhine."

If only it would happen.

"In the pockets...," I began, and waited while he sat on the edge of the mattress and ate the cheese and the potato.

He held out the apple for me.

I smiled. "No. What would my grandmother say?" I whispered, even though the walls were thick and the German was on the other side of the house.

He whispered too. "What would I have done without you and your grandmother?"

"Philippe is trying to get help for you." I looked at him carefully. "Do you trust him?"

Rémy shrugged. "We can't trust anyone. But maybe he'll find a courier. He might have been the one to help my mother and sister." He hesitated, his voice thick. "If only they're safe. If only I'll see them again."

"You will. Someday," I said it fiercely, as if I believed this terrible time wouldn't last.

"Someday," he echoed, then said, "My father," and stopped, his mouth unsteady.

I dug my fingers into my own father's initials, and we listened to sleet, like pebbles, hitting the window. How terrible for Rémy to be alone without anyone to talk to, without a book to read!

"You have to go now," he said. He opened the window and helped me out. As I reached with my feet for the window below, he put his hand on my head.

I couldn't look up; the sleet was sharp against my head. My foot slipped on the icy tiles, and Rémy grabbed my hand, holding me until I slid farther down. Moments later, I reached my window, terrified that I'd see Fürst staring out at me.

*But the door is locked,* I told myself. I raised the icy window and went inside, wiping my hands and legs on the quilt—*Sorry, Mémé*—and spotted the gloves I'd lost last fall under the bed.

*Flyaway Girl.*

I remembered to pull an old robe out of the armoire and shrugged into it in case the German was in the hall. I unlocked the door, gritting my teeth at the sound.

I went downstairs, the old steps creaking. Without thinking, I threw myself into Mémé's arms at the bottom. She raised her hands to my head and smoothed my hair. *Dear child?* Was that what she said?

I slipped out of my damp shoes and left them in the hall as we went into the kitchen. Mémé made tea without tea. "Even the lemons are gone," she said. "But hot water is beginning to taste fine."

She was right. The steaming water felt wonderful in my mouth, my throat, my chest. And my bed waited for me. Never mind the straw that crackled as I turned. I couldn't wait to sleep.

# eighteen

It was warmer the next morning; icicles dripped from the kitchen window, and a pale sun, like a lemon drop, appeared over the back field.

I sat at the table, yawning, as Mémé brought me a cup of cocoa, so weak it barely had color.

Fürst came into the kitchen and frowned. "Certainly not a nourishing breakfast, Gerta."

Gerta! How harsh that sounded.

I didn't answer. And Mémé kept her eyes on the hearth. Didn't he know how little food we had? That we were always hungry?

"That cat," he said. "Always in the way."

Anger filled my chest. Sister gone, the cow, the chickens. And Louis, our beloved Louis. The cat was all we had left.

I clenched my hands into fists and Mémé reached forward, her hands covering them.

He paid no attention. He opened the door, melting snow cascading into the kitchen, and then he was gone, leaving a puddle on the stone floor.

Mémé combed her fingers through my hair. "Oh, Genevieve."

I looked up at her. "Too much. Even though that cat doesn't care one bit about me. She struts around, tail high, as if she owns the place." I tried to smile.

"Sometimes it takes a long time before you earn a cat's trust," Mémé said. "And this cat just wandered in. Who knows what her life was like before."

"Fürst had better not get too close to her. She'll scratch him to pieces. I wish she would."

It was time for school, and I knew I had to be there. "Katrin will be waiting," I said, wiping my eyes.

Mémé nodded. "You found your gloves."

"They were under the bed, waiting for me."

Her lips moved a little. Almost a smile. But she looked as tired as I was.

I went out the door and Tiger darted in. At the end of the path, I looked up, staring at the attic window. Somewhere inside, Rémy waited. I hoped he was warm enough; I hoped he wasn't too hungry.

Katrin came along, books in her arms, her woolen hat pulled low over her forehead.

The snow had melted on the wall, and I motioned to her to sit with me. "Just for a minute." We eased ourselves down on the damp stones, and I stretched my legs out, trying to think of where to start.

She frowned. "Something's happened?"

"Rémy's in the attic."

Eyes wide, she glanced toward the house, even though she couldn't see the window from where we sat.

I told her everything, rushing along breathlessly: climbing on the roof, a courier to take Rémy's mother and sister to Switzerland, that maybe there'd be one for him.

I lowered my head. "But Philippe. I think he's a German sympathizer."

"How can that be?"

"To begin with, I'm almost sure he has my brother's sweater. Why?"

She stared up at the trees along the path. "He might have found it somewhere." She glanced at me sympathetically.

"I'm so afraid . . . , " I began, and stopped. I couldn't say anything more.

We sat there a little longer; we'd be late for school, but neither of us cared.

I saw tears in her eyes. "They're rebuilding the railroad station and the tracks. They're talking about drafting boys," she said. "I can't stop thinking about it. Alsatian boys. My brother, Karl, isn't even seventeen yet."

She stared down at her books. "I thought the Germans weren't terrible. But every day there's something new. My grandfather can't even wear a beret anymore. There's a six months' prison sentence for that." She wiped her eyes. "Berets are too French."

I put my arms around her, feeling how thin she'd become. She was hungry; we were all hungry. "I'm really sorry," I told her.

She shook herself. "But you need help. Who can really trust Monsieur Philippe, now that I think of it? He's always staring out his window, watching what goes on. That old thief. He probably stole the sweater for himself."

I had to grin at her words, *old thief*! But Philippe's head wouldn't even fit into one of André's sweaters!

"We'll just have to watch him," she said. "See what he's up to."

I nodded. "After school."

"We'll go right into the bookshop. I have a few francs. I'll buy a book; you'll sneak around. Why not?"

My mouth went dry. I could think of a dozen reasons not to be sneaking around Philippe's bookshop. I pictured him raising a huge foot and stepping on me.

We were really late, the last ones to slip into the classroom. Herr Albert looked up, tapping his pencil on the desk. "I want to see you both after school today."

"Yes, Herr Albert," Katrin said, answering for us both.

I sank into my seat, terrified. He was a true German, a Nazi. It was almost as if he might have leaned over the stone wall and heard all the things I'd told Katrin. Didn't he say he'd find out everything?

I spent the day worrying about Rémy, worrying about Katrin, worrying about myself. What did Herr Albert know?

"Are you talking to yourself, *Fraülein?*"

I jumped. He stood in front of me. "Sorry," I managed. Everyone looked sympathetic. Liane's fingers curled over an imaginary piano. Claude slammed a book on his desk. And Katrin shook her head, knowing what I was thinking.

As soon as Herr Albert marched to the front of the room, I sank back into my world of worry. What did he want? What could he do to us this afternoon?

At last the day was over. We waited while Herr Albert left the room. He didn't return for at least five minutes.

Katrin leaned over. "He wants to frighten us."

He swooped back into the classroom. "To be punctual is the German way," he said. "You'll each write an essay for me."

That was all?

"You'll call it 'The History of Alsace.' I'll see it the day after Christmas. I'll be here even though the school is closed."

We nodded, escaping down the hall, holding in our laughter. "What happened to 'Merry Christmas'!" Katrin sputtered.

We hesitated at the bookshop, staring at the German books in the window. Two soldiers were inside. One of them was perched on the edge of the counter. He pushed at his little round glasses, laughing at something

Philippe said. The other's back was toward us, his fingers running along, searching for something.

Katrin pushed the door open.

I saw the surprise on Philippe's face as we walked toward him. I was sure he wanted to tell us to go away, to leave him alone with the soldiers. He went to the cluttered table at the side of the room.

Katrin followed him. "You know what books I have, I think."

Philippe barely nodded; he stared at me.

"What shall I get next?" Katrin's voice was so loud that one of the soldiers glanced at her.

"There." Katrin went to a bookcase in the corner. "On the bottom shelf. A book about writing."

Philippe bent down to see where she was pointing. It wasn't easy for him, a large man in such a small space.

Hardly breathing, I ducked behind the curtain into the back room. My eyes swept over the table, the chairs. I slid open one of the cabinet drawers, and then another, all filled with old books and papers.

My hand was on the third drawer when I saw a gray sweater hanging from a hook near the bottom of the stairs. I was reaching out, my hand on the wool, when

I heard Philippe's heavy footsteps coming toward the back.

I pulled the sweater off the hook. If I could just see the zipper and the edge of the sleeves!

Philippe pushed the curtain aside. "What are you doing?"

Behind him, one of the soldiers watched us. "Have you lost something?" he asked.

A soldier with freckles. A soldier who might have been André's age. He was the one who'd taken Sister, the one who'd been sorry. He remembered who I was and smiled, but I looked away.

"I thought there were more books back here."

"No." Philippe couldn't have looked angrier. He glanced at the sweater in my arms. "We don't sell sweaters," he said, and reached for it.

I felt the heavy wool go through my hands even as I tried to hold on to it.

He brushed the collar with one large hand, then hung it back on the hook. He motioned me to the front.

I went past him, past the German, going toward Katrin, who was still at the bookcase, with two or three books in her arms.

The soldier with the glasses pointed to a pile of

books. "Ah, *Mein Kampf,* by Adolf Hitler, our *Führer.* If only more people were like you, Herr Philippe, recognizing our great leader."

I glanced at Katrin and she looked back at me. She put the books on top of the bookcase. "Maybe next time," she told Philippe.

He wasn't paying attention. The German was still talking. I heard him say something, maybe *Let's get together to talk.* I waved at Katrin, wanting to get out of there before the soldiers left and we were alone with Philippe.

She wasn't in a hurry. She pulled her hat tighter around her ears and buttoned her coat slowly.

We started across the square, and she touched my shoulder. "You're right, Genevieve. We both heard the soldier talking as if he were a friend."

And Philippe knew about Rémy, hungry and hidden in our attic!

"Tell me," Katrin said. "Did you find the sweater?"

I shook my head. "A gray sweater. Maybe..." I shrugged. "If only I'd had another few minutes."

It was too late. I might never know.

# nineteen

Mémé and I decorated a tiny pine tree for Christmas but left the wire-whiskered cat hanging in the window to guard us. There'd be no goose this year, but Mémé managed potato pancakes and a small bowl of stewed apples with cinnamon for our dessert.

"A feast," I told her, and upstairs Rémy thought so too, wolfing it all down.

Fürst was having a real feast: dinner at the village hall with the other soldiers, pork and sauerkraut, and a flaming peach tart. Eating food that belonged to the farmers, maybe even to us.

The next morning, I finished my essay for Herr Albert and went off to Katrin's so we could bring them to him together.

But she was sick, lying on the couch, coughing, her face red with fever, her voice hoarse.

I'd have to go alone, bringing both essays with me. I dreaded going into the empty building, facing that man who was angry most of the time. Who knew what he'd say about my miserable handwriting, my paper that had three ink blots?

Inside, Herr Albert sat at his desk, reading. He snapped the book shut. "Fraülein Meyer." His voice was sharp and cold.

"I have Katrin Moeller's work with me too," I told him. "She was too sick to leave her house."

He didn't answer. He held his hand out for the papers and read hers first, shaking his head. It was no better than mine, I guessed. And mine was a mess. I'd made up some of the dates, guessed at the rest. He barely looked at each page before he tossed it on his desk.

I stood there, on one foot and then the other, waiting for him to tell me I could go.

Instead he glared at me, eyes narrowed. "Not much thought went into this work."

What could I say? He was right.

He stacked the few pages neatly, then cleared his throat. "You have a German officer living in your house. Not everyone is that fortunate."

I didn't answer. My face must have told him what I was thinking.

"Ah," he said. "Some students would be going through the officer's things, trying to find out"—he shrugged—"whatever they could for the Resistance."

"I'd never do that."

"That would certainly be against the Germans," he said.

What a horrible man he was! "Can I go now?"

He waved his hand. I was almost at the door when he said something else. *"Carpe diem."*

I knew what that meant. *Seize the day,* something Aunt Marie often said. But there was another string of Latin words. I paid no attention. I almost skipped down the hall. I was free. I didn't have to see him; I didn't have to think about school, or *carpe diem,* or any of that nonsense for another few days. I could concentrate on Rémy. If only I were sure Philippe would send help for him. Every day that the Germans didn't arrive to arrest him surprised me. But no matter what I said to Mémé, she stood firm. Rémy would stay with us, and Philippe would find a courier for him.

I hurried back to the farm. Even with the mittens Mémé had knitted for me, my hands were cold.

Herr Albert would still be sitting in the classroom, probably thinking of all the things he could do next week to make our lives miserable!

I stopped short in the middle of the road.

The rest of what he'd said after *carpe diem.*

If only I could remember what Aunt Marie would have said next. Wasn't it something like *Never mind the consequences?*

I began to walk again, slowly now, trying to remember exactly what he'd said.

A strange man. I put my head back, looking at the treetops, black against a pewter sky. Then my hand in the mitten went to my mouth when I realized that he'd been telling me to look through Fürst's things for anything I might find. *Seize the day. Never mind the consequences.*

*Sometimes people surprise you,* something Aunt Marie said.

I was surprised. More than surprised.

The bare branches grated against each other. *Some students would be going through the officer's things... It would be against the Germans ... it would be for the Resistance.*

Was Herr Albert part of the Resistance?

Marching around the room, putting up the German flag. It was all an act!

I began to walk again; then I ran. For the first time, I cared about doing something for Herr Albert. And something else made my heart sing. He'd believed I'd understand what he was saying.

I went up the walk, the wire-whiskered cat in the window, wondering if I should tell Mémé what had happened.

Maybe not. At least, not yet.

In the kitchen, candles lay on the counter; the cellar door was open. She must be downstairs, and Fürst was off in the village somewhere, so I went upstairs.

His door was locked. Of course. I went down the stairs two at a time and reached into the small kitchen drawer that was filled with keys, some of them black with age. But I knew what I was looking for: the ring of keys I'd often seen Mémé use.

Fürst kept the room the same way Mémé did: the quilt stretched neatly across the bed, his clothes hidden away in the armoire. I looked under the bed, went through the dresser drawers, opened the armoire doors and went through his pockets. I found only a scrap of paper, written in German: *sugar, flour, butter, eggs, cream, chocolate.*

A grocery list.

Nothing more.

Then came the sound of the motorcycle.

I stood in the doorway, making sure I hadn't disturbed anything. The armoire doors were closed, the quilt straight on the bed.

Quickly, my hands shaking, I locked the door and raced back to the kitchen to put the keys in the drawer. I went down to the cellar to help Mémé with whatever she was doing, probably gathering up the few potatoes that were left. The steps were steep, but she never stopped, never gave up.

# twenty

$\mathcal{It}$ was a strange afternoon, no school, no outside work, and Mémé had taken a nap. Mémé sleeping in the daytime! But then, her ankle had never healed the way it should have. She held on to railings, to chairs as she passed.

Fürst carried things downstairs; he looped a small case over the handlebars of his motorcycle, a uniform on a hanger; then he sped away.

I spent the rest of the day with Rémy, bringing him food, more water, a third sweater and a book I'd found in Mémé's living room.

He was tired and bored. "What takes Philippe so long?" he asked. "I can't stay here forever."

I bit my lip and left him, promising I'd ask. Downstairs, I read another book I'd found on Mémé's shelf, but it was hard to concentrate.

Later, I opened the kitchen door to see Fürst at the table, digging a fork into a plate of potatoes sprinkled with nutmeg. It was probably my dinner, or Rémy's.

"Ah, Fraülein Meyer," he said. "You're home in time to say good-bye. I'll be leaving in a few minutes."

I glanced at Mémé, who raised her eyebrows.

"I have a promotion." He waved his hand over the potatoes. "This is a celebration."

*Leaving!*

Yes. A small leather suitcase rested on the floor next to him. It was the beginning of a new year, maybe a new beginning for us.

"Your grandmother has been a good host." He shoveled in a huge mouthful of potatoes. "Everything is clean in the good German way, but she's a little stingy with the food and the coal."

I thought of the carrots she'd managed to find in the field yesterday. She'd scraped and chopped them with an onion she'd saved. "Eat," she'd told me, "I'm not hungry."

Her clothes hung on her; her hands were almost transparent.

He said it again. "Stingy."

I saw something in Mémé's eyes. Warning me?

Realizing the anger that was boiling up from my chest into my throat?

"She's wonderful!" I almost yelled it, and slammed the book on the table, just missing his plate of potatoes.

He jumped.

I stamped past into the hall.

"An ungainly girl," he said after me.

"No." Surprisingly, Mémé's voice was as angry as mine had been. "I couldn't get along without her during this terrible time." She broke off and began again. "Her father would have been proud of her."

I glanced into the kitchen; her back was toward me, bent, thin, her hair steel gray in a tight bun.

I leaned against the wall.

*She'd said no. She'd said she couldn't do without me.* I swallowed.

*Once, she'd said: You may come again after the war.*

*She'd called me dear child.*

And my father. *He would have been proud of me.*

Words I'd never forget.

*Sometimes people surprise you.*

I was beginning to love Mémé.

I heard the sound of a motor and peered out the hall window. A black car, long and sleek, two small Nazi flags flying on the hood, was parked outside. Waiting to take him away.

The kitchen chair scraped back, and I craned my head to see him shrug into his coat and reach for the suitcase under the table. "Thank you, Frau Meyer," he said. "I hope to see you one day. Perhaps when we're all at peace."

He stepped out the door, and the cat raked his boot, darted inside, and slid under the table. Then Fürst was gone, the motor purring as the car sped away. If we were lucky, we'd never see him again.

Mémé slid his plate into the sink. "We were foolish, Genevieve. If the car hadn't come for him just then, who knows what he would have done?"

At my feet, the cat scratched my leg, and then she was up and in my lap. I reached out slowly, my hand on her head. I didn't move. I looked at Mémé, tears in my eyes.

"Your cat," she said.

"Yes."

I sat there for long minutes until the cat must have decided she'd had enough. She went to the door and I let her out.

But I had things to do. "Rémy doesn't have to stay

in the attic!" I danced around the table. "And Louis can come home."

Mémé nodded. "You make me dizzy."

And one more thing. The painting.

Mémé followed as I went up the stairs to my old bedroom. I crawled up on the roof, tapping the window, seeing Rémy's face, wavery in the old glass.

"The German is gone," I called in to him. "You can come inside where it's warm."

We slid down and came into the bedroom, and, almost not believing how daring I was, I put my arms around him, careful not to hurt his burn, which had begun to scab over. I danced with him too, both of us laughing, as Mémé watched.

I went back up for the painting and managed it carefully until I reached the bedroom window again.

"Let me," I told Mémé, and smiled at Rémy, who sat on the edge of the bed.

She stood at her bedroom door as I took down the ugly watercolor of the Vosges Mountains, then slid the painting out of the pillowcase, wiping the frame gently on my skirt. I reached up and hung it on the wall where it belonged.

I stared at the two girls, their faces beautiful, huge

black bows on their long hair, and leaned forward, leaned closer.

"Oh." It was almost a breath.

"So you see it this time," Mémé said.

I couldn't answer.

"Yes," she said. "I realized it the moment you stepped off the train with André that summer."

In the painting Mémé was beautiful, and I knew I wasn't. I hadn't even thought I was pretty, but still, she could have been me.

I thought of my father, then Mémé starving herself so I could eat. I thought of her father, who'd made the wooden shoe. And André's voice one time: *Long ago we were Alsatian.*

"Miel," I said.

Her hand went to her mouth. "Your grandfather's name for me."

We collected Rémy from my room and went downstairs into the kitchen. Before we could sit at the table, Mémé glanced at the armoire. "It's time to move it."

Food!

Rémy and I managed to push the armoire aside. We brought jars of thick white beans, tomato sauce, golden pears and fat sausages to the table.

We didn't talk. Instead we feasted, forks to our mouths, the beans in their rich sauce sliding down our throats.

We sat there as it grew dark outside; then Mémé took Rémy into the downstairs bedroom while I washed the plates and let them drain on the counter.

Mémé came back and stood at the kitchen door, looking out at the darkness. I knew she was thinking about Louis.

"I'll go," I said, and dropped one of the pewter plates. It clattered across the floor and came to rest under the table. "Sorry," I muttered. I scooped it up and grabbed my jacket before she could say anything, and went past her at the door.

It was a beautiful night; a huge moon had come up that was almost orange. It lighted the back of the house and the fields. I walked quickly, though, anxious to bring the dog to Mémé.

I climbed the stone wall and went through the trees until I saw the small house in front of me. The door opened before I could raise my hand to knock.

"Louis heard you." The woodcutter pulled me inside. "Are you all right?"

"The German is gone," I said.

Louis was right behind him, looking up, whining, his tail wagging hard. I leaned over to run my hand along his back.

"Ah," the woodcutter said. "I'm glad. The dog has been sad, wanting to go home."

But Louis had been well cared for. A thick mat was in front of a table, a bowl of water and a plate with bits of food was left in the corner.

The woodcutter had been carving what looked like a chess set. Small figures lay on that table: a queen, maybe, and a row of pawns. I wanted to stop and look, but Louis stood at the door, tail down, worried that he wouldn't get to go home.

"Thank you," I told the woodcutter. "We're grateful. More than you can know."

I leaned over the dog. "Time to go home."

Louis bounded out, looking back at me, almost as if he were telling me to hurry.

Mémé waited at the door, and he rushed to her, crying. Her arms went around him, and I saw that she had tears in her eyes. But she said only, "Time for bed."

# twenty-one

*For* the next few days it was as if the war had never been. School had begun again after the holidays, and I could almost ignore the soldiers who seemed to be everywhere. I couldn't ignore Herr Albert, though. He strutted around the room or stood in front, hands behind his back. I watched him, wondering what he was like before the war when he didn't have to act his way through the day.

In the late afternoons Louis lay under the table, his muzzle on my feet, content to be home, while Mémé crocheted a sweater from old wool, interrupting herself to show me cable stitches for the socks I was knitting.

And yet we were wary. Things seemed almost too quiet. Wouldn't the Germans still be searching for Rémy?

Today I'd managed to stop at Philippe's to find out what was happening with the courier, then went back to Rémy and Mémé. Philippe had said, "Soon. It's dangerous work; it takes time."

My hands were fists. "It's taking too long. I don't believe him."

"Oh, Genevieve."

"Philippe lies. I know he does."

Mémé leaned forward. "What is this all about?"

"He has André's sweater."

"That can't be."

"Oh, it can be. I think I saw it. Really." I waved my hand in front of my face. "Somehow he saw André doing something that summer, and told the Germans. Maybe André never got to the ship; he could be in prison now, right here."

"Ah, Genevieve, your imagination is boundless." Mémé sighed. "Let me tell you about the Great War. Gérard sat exactly where you are. We'd both been up all night. Remember, our village was German then, and the French needed to take it because of the garrison filled with soldiers at the edge of the square. They needed guides."

I sat up. My father in this chair, as tired as I was.

"We waited until it was dark and managed to sneak through the village. Philippe stood at the window, watching. We went toward the mountains, Gérard and I, and two others. We were seen and the Germans came after us, yelling: 'Traitors!' We knew if they caught us..."

She broke off, staring up at the ceiling, tears on her cheeks.

"What happened?"

She shook her head. "Another time. We have to have dinner."

We sat there, eating until we were full. But as we finished, I heard the sound of a motor. A truck? Mémé and I pushed our chairs back from the table. Rémy stood, almost like a deer, ready to run.

Mémé pointed. "The cellar."

He moved quickly; his footsteps on the stairs were whispers of sound. His winter jacket was looped over his chair; I threw it under the table.

The armoire was still away from the wall, but there was no time to do anything about it. Mémé slid Rémy's plate under hers. We sat there, frozen, as the sharp rap came on the outside door.

Mémé raised her head, straightened herself, then opened it.

Two soldiers came into the kitchen, looking around. One reached across the table, sweeping plates and food onto the floor. "Where is he?"

Mémé's face was calm. "My husband has been dead for many years."

The other soldier went behind the armoire. "They're hoarding food," he said. "A good find. We'll take it all with us."

At the table, the soldier leaned forward. "We know he's here."

Mémé looked around. "There are only the two of us."

One of the soldiers climbed the stairs toward the bedrooms. The painting!

His partner opened doors: the pantry, the bedroom and then the stairs to the cellar. He pulled a flashlight off his belt and started down.

The cellar was huge, I told myself, and even with the flashlight, maybe Rémy was hidden. I leaned forward against the table, my knees tight together to stop their trembling, my feet on his jacket, pushing it farther under the table.

Across from me, Mémé sat unmoving, her thin hands clenched.

The soldier who'd been upstairs clattered into the kitchen, shaking his head. "We'll find him," he said, his boots on the food we'd been eating. The rest, which would have lasted us until the next harvest, would be gone. But he hadn't seen the painting, or if he had, he wasn't interested.

And like a miracle, the second one came up from the cellar. "No one is there."

They went out the door, the motor started up and the sound of the truck gradually faded away.

I tried to stand, but I felt as if my legs wouldn't hold me. And so we sat at the table waiting, thinking Rémy would appear.

But he didn't come.

Mémé sighed. "Genevieve, perhaps . . ."

On shaky legs, I went down the stairs, calling his name softly. The cellar was the width of the house, with many small rooms almost like caves. I went back and forth, stopping, listening. But even in the darkness, I could tell he wasn't there. And in back, over my head, an open window rattled, pulling in cold air.

How had the German not seen it? I shook my head. They hadn't seen the jacket either.

Rémy had saved himself, and us, and was some-where outside in the shelter of the trees, or maybe at the woodcutter's place.

Back up in the kitchen, I pulled his jacket out from under the table. "I'm going to look for him," I told Mémé.

She looked doubtful, but she said, "Yes. Go slowly. Watch."

As the sky inched toward darkness, I slipped between the trees, until I saw the dim shape of the woodcutter's house. The door was open.

I stood there, shocked. The woodcutter was gone, and inside the room the quilt had been thrown from the bed onto the floor, the rocking chair splintered, the table with carved figures overturned. Small carving knives were on the floor, along with a cup of blue paint, which had splashed over the table legs.

I thought of the happy day with Rémy and André, riding the bicycles in the sun, the tower with its storks' nest, the blue-gray house nearby.

Shirmeck Prison was in my mind, or worse, Struthof, the terrible concentration camp that people whispered about.

I went out the door, hurrying through the forest, fearful now that soldiers still might be watching the woodcutter's house. *Philippe,* I thought bitterly.

We spent the next hour cleaning up the food on the floor and pushed the empty armoire back against the wall. Then we waited. Would Rémy come back? I was sure he wouldn't.

I hoped he'd found a warm place to stay. But I couldn't imagine what to do with his jacket. If the Germans came again, if they found it, what trouble we'd be in.

I wrapped it in a small quilt that was old and frayed around the edges and stood with it in my arms.

"Bury it," Mémé said.

"Suppose Rémy comes back for it?"

She shook her head. "We'll find something else for him. We can't take a chance."

I knew she was right. I found a shovel in the barn, but outside the ground was rock-hard, still frozen from the snow.

I went back to the barn and climbed the ladder to the loft, pushing the jacket ahead of me, and buried it deep under the hay.

The best I could do, I told myself.

Inside, Mémé was waiting. Tired and worried, we climbed the stairs to our old rooms.

Where was Rémy? Where was the woodcutter?

And then, surprisingly, I slept.

# twenty-two

*Early* the next morning, I awoke suddenly, heart pounding. Something terrible had happened. I jolted up, my mouth dry as dust, my knees shaking. *It was only a dream*, I told myself, *only a nightmare*.

Rémy.

The woodcutter.

Not a dream.

I dressed, braided my hair with trembling fingers and went downstairs. Mémé was stirring a few oats in a pot of boiling water.

"We have to tell Philippe," she said.

"Philippe! How can we trust him? He might have betrayed us."

She closed her eyes. "The Great War. Germans shooting at us, your father down on the ground. I knew

I had to have help. I ran to the village, ran as I never had before, straight to Philippe.

"When we got back to your father, blood had soaked his sleeves, his shirt. Philippe carried him to the farm, good, strong Philippe, telling me he wouldn't let him die. 'Hold on, Gérard,' he'd said. 'Almost home.'"

Mémé looked down at her hands. "Here, in this kitchen, we wrapped Gérard's chest with cloths, and Philippe pressed his hands against the wound until the bleeding stopped. Know this, Genevieve. I'd trust Philippe with my life. With your life.

"He made it possible for us to go on with our work. Gérard healed slowly, still in pain, but we were able to lead the French into villages we knew and fight against the Germans."

I sat there, picturing her young, as fierce as I saw her now. I had to do something too. "Oh, Mémé. I have to look for Rémy."

"You can't do that. You have to go to school. It must seem that you hardly knew Rémy or the wood-cutter." She leaned forward, the lines deep in her forehead. "Someone has betrayed them, and us, just as someone betrayed your father that night long ago."

I closed my eyes.

Katrin?

Was that possible?

"I will go to Philippe myself," she said, "and tell him . . ."

"I could . . . ," I began. But suppose it had been Katrin? How could I leave her on the way to school to go to the bookshop?

I went outside and walked toward her house. She was the only one who knew that Rémy was with us. Our friendship was over. I'd tell her that.

Katrin called from her doorway. "Genevieve? I'm not going to school today." Her voice was filled with tears. "My brother is being sent to work in a factory somewhere. We'll go to the station with him."

Blowing up the tracks had all been for nothing. The Germans had forced men to repair them.

I ran across the field, back to the kitchen, to tell Mémé I was early, that I'd go to Philippe. And then I was on the road, hurrying to the village square.

The sign on the bookshop door read CLOSED. It was early, after all.

I flew around to the back. Through the window, I saw Philippe at the table and rapped hard enough to hurt my knuckles.

He opened the door; I stumbled in and slid down at the table, too breathless to say a word.

He went back to the window, pulled down the shade and sat awkwardly, almost as if it were an effort to fit his huge bulk in that narrow chair. He stared at me, waiting.

"Mémé trusts you," I said.

"And why not? We grew up together, fought underground during the Great War . . ."

"They came for Rémy last night."

He leaned forward.

"They didn't find him, I think. But the woodcutter . . . I'm not sure. They've ruined his house." My voice trembled as I raised my shoulders.

Philippe shook his head. "Perhaps the courier will come. He is on his way back from . . ." His voice trailed off. He went to the window and raised the shade just enough to peer out.

"Finish what you started to say," I said, stopping myself just before I banged my fist on the table.

"The less you know, the better. How do we know we can trust you? An American—"

I held up my hand to cut him off. "I know what I am."

He sighed. "How old are you?"

"Sixteen." Not true, of course, but I was tall for fourteen, and how would he know what class I was in?

He shrugged his huge shoulders. Then he sighed. "The couriers know the way to Switzerland, or even west to Spain. They've learned which houses are safe. But still, it's dangerous. We just have to wait, to hope."

He went to a small stove at the side of the room and poured hot water into a cup. "Would you like coffee?"

"Coffee?" Where had he gotten coffee? It had disappeared months ago.

"Coffee without coffee." He poured hot water into two cups.

He reached for the door of a cabinet and pulled out a sweater. He shoved it across the table in front of me.

It wasn't André's. It wasn't even the same sweater I'd seen the other day: not a zipper in front, but wooden buttons, no raveling at the hem. It was meant for a large man, a man like Philippe.

"A lie," I said bitterly, pushing the sweater away from me.

"Like your age." For the first time he laughed, a

dry laugh, almost without sound. "Go to school, Gene-vieve. Forget about war for a while."

I went out to the alley, slamming the door behind me, with enough force that I almost broke the window.

That afternoon, on the way home, I saw Katrin and her mother walking all the way from the railway station. I remembered Madame Moeller saying, *We were Germans before. We'll have to be Germans.*

And their names hadn't been changed. German names: Katrin. Karl. Moeller.

How had I told Katrin everything?

I caught up with them as they turned onto the path toward their farm. "Katrin?"

Her mother kept going. Maybe she was crying.

"Will we ever see Karl again?" Katrin said. "Will we ever see any of them? Dozens of boys on the train platform..."

"You told someone."

"About Karl leaving? Everyone knows that."

"About Rémy and the woodcutter. About all the things I told you."

She looked away. "I didn't tell anyone."

"You're lying."

She turned back to me, her face shocked.

I grabbed her arm, held it hard. "Who?"

She was really crying now. "I didn't—"

"Yes, you did."

"I have to go inside." Her cheeks were blotched. "My mother is waiting for me."

I moved in front of her, blocking the way. "We'll stay here forever, until you tell me."

"You're as bad as the Germans."

"Worse," I said.

"The only one I told was Liane."

Liane, who played an imaginary piano on her desk.

"And maybe Claude."

Madame Jacques's son from the pâtisserie.

"You can trust them," she said. "They'd never—"

I let go of her arm. "Go inside to your mother. You're not my friend. I'll never walk to school with you again. Never tell you..." I took a breath. "Never tell you anything."

I went back down the path. It was beginning to rain, and even in my warm coat I was shivering.

# twenty-three

Mémé was outside, her hair wet, her jacket soaked, staring at the field, which was only now beginning to thaw.

"Come inside," I said.

She looked up, wiping her hands on her apron, and we went across the gravel path into the kitchen. I tossed my coat and hat on an empty chair and my books on the countertop. "I've done something terrible," I said.

She slid the teakettle over the flame and stood there waiting for the water to boil.

"You're not paying attention to me. I've done something terrible."

She turned. "How can I not pay attention to you, Genevieve? You are everywhere. Your books, your clothes, even your bathrobe can be found in every room of this house."

She pulled two of the Strasbourg cups from the

armoire. "In the beginning," she said, "I thought I'd go out of my mind. An old woman used to a neat house, to a quiet house. Instead I have dishes in the sink; there's clattering on the stairs, doors slamming."

I bent my head. I wanted to tell her that at home our house wasn't like a tomb, that Aunt Marie sang, recited poetry in French, that sometimes I had friends over and we made fudge.

I didn't say anything. I didn't have time.

Mémé put the steaming water in front of me. "But after a while, I remembered your father, the noise he made, the messes!"

I closed my eyes: *His notebook with the terrible marks, the doodles, the list of his classmates, Suzanne the tattletale, the initials G.M. cut into the attic floor, my father, meringues his favorite.*

"I told Katrin everything," I said. "And she told Liane and Claude. It's my fault. All of it." I swiped at the tears running down my cheeks.

Mémé bent her head so I could see that stiff part in her hair. "Sometimes things happen that we'd never expected, that we never thought about," she said slowly. "But the important thing is to begin again."

She went into the hall and brought back my father's

picture. "You see how sad he looks. He had to leave everything he loved. Some of our friends had been taken away, but he had managed to escape, and would cross the country to Spain." Her lips were unsteady. "And then to America."

Sad? All the times I'd looked at the picture. *Grim. Angry. Unfriendly. Miserable.* Never once had I thought *sad.* But there it was exactly. His dark eyes staring out, his hands clenched.

My Alsatian father, Gérard. Sad.

"That day, Philippe took his picture with a box camera so I'd have something to remember him by. Gérard blamed himself. 'I must have told someone, Maman,' he said." Mémé shrugged her thin shoulders. "We never knew who it was."

I ran my fingers over the picture. I knew how he felt. If someone took a picture of me now, they'd see the same sorrow, the same grief.

"Drink your tea without tea," Mémé said. "Raise your head."

I couldn't drink, I couldn't speak. My throat felt as if it were closing.

"It is useless to blame yourself." Her voice was harsh. "There is much more to this than Katrin."

I glanced at her. I could almost count her bones. Her dress hung loosely around her. She weighed less than I did now, and came only to my shoulder.

"We do what we can," she said.

And what she could do was run this farm by herself. She had worked in the resistance during the Great War. In this war, she had sheltered Rémy. She had taken in a girl who was forgetful and messy, who hadn't loved her.

She must have known what I was thinking. "A girl who changed my life," she said. "A girl who looked like me when I was young, who acted like the son I loved."

Her arms went across the table. I could see the veins running through her small hands. I reached for them, held them in mine.

We sat there, not speaking; then she gave my hand a quick pat and picked up her cup. "Drink, child," she said. "Your tea is getting cold."

And that's what I did. I raised the cup to my mouth; the water was still hot, comforting.

I sipped it slowly. *We do what we can,* she'd said.

And so I was determined to find Rémy.

# twenty-four

That Sunday, a cold January morning, I woke to find Louis on the floor next to me and Tiger curled up at the bottom of the bed. I lay there, trying not to move my feet; the irritable cat was close enough to pounce on my toes.

And then I remembered. Rémy!

I took a chance, slid my legs over the side of the bed quickly and dressed, my fingers fumbling with the buttons. I had only today to look for Rémy without thinking about school.

Church was first, so I had a late start. Afterward, I hurried around to the barn and pulled open the doors. Tiger darted in ahead of me, ready to search for a tasty mouse or two. I shuddered. I knew Louis was eating rats now.

Enough snow had melted so I could ride the bicycle. I wheeled it out, my eyes going to the Vosges Mountains in the distance, then closer where the woods led to the village. Rémy was somewhere, I told myself.

The handlebars were freezing! I rested the bike against the wall and poked my head in the door.

Mémé looked up.

"I'm going to look for—" I began.

She broke in. "If the Germans can't find him, why do you think you might?"

"I don't know. I have to try." I could hear the desperation in my voice.

"Eat something first," she said.

I began to shake my head, but I was so hungry. I needed something. Still in my coat and hat, I stood in the kitchen, where somehow Mémé had managed to make warm cereal. I spooned it up, wondering if there was enough for her, or had she given me all of it? If I ever made it home, I'd send her food, tons of food, I promised myself.

She stood there, watching me. "Stay away from the main roads. If you're stopped, you might say you're looking for food. Be home before—"

Was that worry on her face? I waved my hand, cutting her off. "Dark. I know." I wiped my mouth as she reached for the empty bowl. "I'll be all right."

Would I really be all right? Wandering around in the woods, when the Germans were everywhere?

*My fault. All my fault.*

I pulled my woolen hat down to cover my ears, then went along the road. Even the Germans weren't around on this Sunday afternoon.

By the time I reached the village, I realized I should have pumped up the tires. Riding up the hills was hard.

I began to see the dark trucks of the Germans far ahead. Where was I going? I wasn't even sure.

I passed stubbled fields, still winter gray, and turned down a side road, which was mostly dirt and gravel with a few patches of snow here and there.

The road came to an end, and almost in front of me was a German soldier, his hand raised. Guarding the field in back of him?

The sign on the fence: VERBOTEN. Forbidden.

I slid to a stop, the old bike veering to one side, wobbling, then caught in the mud. My heart ticked up in my throat. Could I turn the bike and ride away before he took the ten steps to get to me?

I'd never be able to do it.

Then I saw who he was: André's age, freckled face,

the one who'd been sorry about Sister, the one who'd been looking for books at Philippe's.

I straddled the bike. I didn't move, and neither did he. We stared at each other. Over his shoulder, I saw a horse in the field. She tossed her head; her back rippled.

I caught my breath. Sister, looking fine! I remembered André teaching me to harness her. I'd held apples for her. Lumps of sugar.

The soldier walked toward me. "You're not supposed to be here."

I tried to turn the bike, head down. He was German, after all. A soldier. The enemy.

He was in front of me now. "You wanted to see the horse?"

I shook my head. "I didn't know she was here."

He looked past me, along the road. "She belongs to an officer now. But would you like to go to her?"

I felt a flash of anger. "She's my grandmother's horse."

"Of course. And someday, maybe . . . But stay for only a few minutes. The officer will be here soon."

He opened the gate, then steadied the bicycle as I went past him and crossed the field, calling the horse.

She saw me and came toward me, hoping for a treat.

If only I'd had something to give her. If only I could take her out of there and bring her to Mémé.

I ran my hand over Sister's back, reached up to feel her muzzle with its stiff dark hairs. Someday.

"*Fraülein*," the German called.

I gave the horse one last pat, crossed the field again and closed the gate behind me. I didn't look at him as I took the bike and steadied it.

"I'm sorry," he said.

I turned the bike, and he said it again. "I'm really sorry."

The anger burst from my chest. "You're part of it. I wouldn't be here, we wouldn't be hungry, people evacuated, Jews deported . . ."

I bit off the name *Rémy*.

I didn't bother to look at him as I pedaled away. I knew he was looking after me.

It wasn't until I was past that road, onto the next small path, sheltered by the forest, that I stopped the bike and leaned it against a tree.

I crouched down, my head on my knees, shaking, the anger gone, feeling so sad. But I couldn't stay there for long. I had to keep searching. I had to find Rémy.

The rest of the day went by slowly as I went from

one hidden path to another, almost too tired to keep going on those tires that were almost flat. My feet were sore, beginning to blister.

It was dark by the time I found my way back to the farm. I passed Katrin's house with its red roof and looked away.

Mémé stood in the doorway, her hand on Louis's head, the cat stretching in front of her. "Genevieve?"

I shook my head. "He's nowhere."

I dropped the bicycle on the gravel path, too tired to put it in the barn. Inside, I slid onto a chair, pulling off my shoes, feeling the pain in my feet, my toes. Mémé put a bowl of thin soup in front of me. It held a few cabbage leaves, another carrot and something that looked like grass, maybe chives. She went back to the stove and poured the rest into a bowl for herself, with a little left for Louis.

I told her about Sister, and she turned. "We couldn't have taken care of her as well as they have."

I breathed in the steam from the soup, wondering if Rémy had eaten today, wondering if he might be with the woodcutter. "We'll have to say I've had the grippe, a terrible sore throat, because I'm not going to give up. I won't go to school tomorrow."

"I knew you wouldn't give up," she said. "You remind me..."

I answered for her. "Of my father?"

She turned back to the stove. "No."

I didn't ask. I knew. I looked away from her, smiling just a little.

Sipping at the soup, I thought of that long day.

Rémy was out there somewhere.

Would I ever find him?

I'd keep looking tomorrow.

# twenty-five

$\mathcal{I}'d$ dreamed last night, a mixed-up dream of my school at home, with its cornerstone that read *1914*. I awoke wondering what my father would have been doing that year, the beginning of the Great War in Europe.

I slid out of bed, in a hurry to get started, but when my feet touched the floor, the pain from the blisters and the muscles in my legs was amazing.

Rocking back and forth, I knew I'd never be able to get on the bike today. I was filled with anger at myself and that old bike.

I hobbled into the kitchen. Mémé was pulling on an ancient jacket that might have belonged to my grandfather. "I'm going out to the field. Maybe I'll find a vegetable or two." She stopped. "What's the matter, child?"

I raised one foot to show her, and she winced. "Sit."

"How can I look for him?" I said bitterly. "I can't even get as far as the road."

"Rest awhile." She went out the door. Did she ever rest?

Katrin was hurrying up the gravel path, head down, her books in her arms. I didn't want her to see my feet, or to know about what I'd been doing. I pulled my robe around me.

Katrin passed Mémé, who was leaving the barn, and came to the kitchen door. I had no choice. "You can come in."

"Are you sick?"

I shrugged.

"Listen, Gen, just for a minute. I went to Liane. I asked her if she'd told anyone about Rémy."

I wrapped the robe tighter around my ankles. "She probably told a dozen people," I said, forgetting that I wasn't going to say a word to her.

I saw her shake her head from the corner of my eye; then I looked toward the window at Mémé disappearing across the field.

"Liane said she was sorry, that she didn't remember what I'd told her. She'd been practicing a Bach piece for church in her head." Katrin reached across the table, but I moved my hands away. "Liane said she knew I was saying something, but she just kept nodding so I wouldn't be disappointed in her."

I swallowed. It sounded like Liane, paying no attention in school, playing an imaginary piano all day. I had to believe Katrin. "But what about Claude?"

"I saw him after school. He was furious with me for asking. 'Do you think I'd give the Germans one thing?' he yelled at me, his face red. 'Do you think I'm not French?'"

"So it was your mother!" I closed my eyes. I didn't want to see the tears in hers.

"Never! And remember, *you* told me, Genevieve!"

She was right.

"I have to go to school," she said. "But think about it. We said we'd be friends forever."

I should have called her back, but I waited too long. By the time I managed to get to the window, walking on the sides of my feet, she was halfway down the path, running. She never heard me.

For a while, I sat in my robe with my bare feet on a kitchen chair, sipping coffee without coffee. I wasn't even hungry.

I sank onto the cold stone floor, holding my ankles,

turning my feet so I could see the thick blisters. If only I could have gone after Katrin. It was too hard even to go back to the table, impossible to go to my room and throw myself on the bed.

After a while, I slept. Maybe that was why I didn't hear the motorcycle rumble up the path and around to the kitchen door.

The banging was loud. I jumped, opening my eyes. Fürst stared in at me.

My heart drummed against my chest. What was he doing here? Never mind the pain. I stood up and hobbled to the door as quickly as I could.

"I'm back, Fraülein Meyer," he said, as if I'd be glad to see him.

I swallowed, nodding.

"What happened to your feet?" He rested his briefcase on one of the chairs and a suitcase on the floor next to him.

"It's nothing." The pain was so bad I could hardly talk.

"I'll require the bedroom again," he said.

The painting! "If you come back later, my grandmother and I will have it ready for you."

He looked around. "Where is she?"

I waved my hand. "Outside somewhere."

"I saw your dog. I wonder where he was when I was here last." He stared at me. "I wonder too where the boy was."

I thought about saying *What boy?* But it was hard to think. Already Fürst was on to food. "I was told about your hoarding food in an armoire," he said. "Food that I was denied." I could hear something in his voice. Fury?

If only I weren't alone here with him.

He shrugged, took a breath. "I'll drop my things off upstairs and be back for dinner tonight."

"The quilt," I said. "The bed . . ."

It was too late. He went around the table and climbed the stairs, carrying his things.

I took three steps to the table and tucked my feet underneath.

What would we do about Louis? What could we do? He'd have to stay here. There was nowhere for him to go.

And what was upstairs? Were there marks on the windowsill from where I'd gone out on the roof? I closed my eyes. He'd see the painting, of course.

His footsteps were on the stairs again. He came into the kitchen, humming, carrying Mémé's painting.

"Please," I said, before I could think. "It's Mémé when she was young."

He stopped humming. "You hid this from me." He propped it up on the table, where I could see Mémé's lovely face. He stared at it. "A fine work. It really wasn't fair of your grandmother to hang that terrible painting of the Vosges in my room." He flicked imaginary dust off the top of the frame. "Selfish. Don't you know the power I have? How important I am?"

"Please," I begged.

"You'll have some paper. We need to wrap this."

I didn't answer.

"Perhaps you'll look, *Fraülein*," he said. "You know what's in these cabinets."

"I don't know . . . ," I began. I did know. Mémé kept wrapping paper in a drawer on the other side of the room.

His voice changed. "Stand up and look."

I put my hands on the table's edge and pushed back the chair. I managed to walk across the room and open the drawer.

I hobbled back to the table and folded the paper around the painting. Would I ever see it again?

"Let me see your foot."

"It's nothing," I said again.

"Do it."

I raised one foot.

"Burned," he said.

I caught my breath, thinking of the explosion at the station. Would he think . . . "I dropped a pot of boiling water."

Perfect. Boiling water, bare feet.

He picked up the painting and went out, the door closing behind him, and sped away on the motorcycle.

I realized he'd left his briefcase upstairs. I counted to fifty, then took the ring of keys and went up to the bedroom on my knees. His briefcase was there, next to the bed. I fiddled with the lock, and it was open. "Ah, Fürst," I whispered. "Not so careful after all."

I searched, papers, numbers, arrests, all in German, of course. And then the name followed by a word: *Rolf, missing.*

Rolf? Rémy?

Two more names. The first: *Woodcutter. Struthof.* My hand went to my mouth: Struthof, the concentration camp. I'd heard it was the only one in all of France. And then: *Albert, the teacher. His house, school? Today.*

I closed my eyes. Herr Albert would be at school.

I closed the case and sat on the stairs, bumping down each step as fast as I could go, my legs stretched out in front of me.

I didn't stop for my coat. I managed to slide into the wooden sabots, then went to the bicycle, crying out with the pain, pedaling down the gravel path away from the farm.

I was just able to hide at the edge of the woods as I heard the motorcycle: Fürst remembering and coming back for his briefcase?

I waited only for a moment, then kept going, feeling the wetness in my socks as blisters broke.

Past the village, at the school, I threw the bicycle down where it couldn't be seen and peered along the empty hall, hearing the voices of students, of teachers.

At the classroom, I raised my fingers to the little window, and of course, Herr Albert saw me.

I beckoned and he came to the door, opened it a few inches and came outside. "You were sick," he said.

"Go," I said. "Leave. They're coming for you. Don't go home. Go to the bookshop."

He pushed me away from the door so I couldn't be seen, then opened it farther, saying, "Go on with your work," to the students.

Herr Albert! Precise even now!

We hurried out of the school building. He stopped to put his hand on my shoulder. "I'm grateful, more than you know," he said. "But not surprised."

"Hurry," I said. "And please tell Monsieur Philippe that the woodcutter was taken to Struthof."

"I'm sorry," Herr Albert said. "Poor man. Try not to be seen as you go back home."

He took the back road to the bookshop, and I pedaled to the farm, my feet pulsing with pain.

# twenty-six

Mémé must have seen me as I pedaled back up the path to the kitchen. She came in from across the field a few minutes later, wiping her feet.

I was at the table, my head down, shivering with cold, in too much pain to find my sweater.

She didn't say a word. She went into the bedroom and hurried back with the quilt, wrapping it around my shoulders. She took her woolen hat off a hook and pulled it down over my head.

"A moment." She put water on to heat and covered my feet with a towel.

"What happened?" she said, still kneeling next to me.

Where could I begin?

The painting!

I tried to get the words out. "I'm sorry. Fürst is back." I swallowed. "He's taken..."

She stared at me. "Of course. He came to the bedroom and found the painting."

"It's my fault."

She looked grim. "You may be guilty of many things, Genevieve, but this is certainly not one of them."

"I know you loved it." My mouth was trembling. "I loved it too."

She put her arms around me. "We will have it back someday. I always meant it for you, from the first time your father wrote and told me how lovely you were. 'A smiling baby,' he said. 'A perfect baby. I can't stop watching her.'"

I began to cry, to sob. "He loved me."

She looked shocked. "Of course. What good father doesn't love his daughter? But more, you and André and your mother had made him happy, so far from home."

She wiped the tears on my face with her small fingers. "Later we'll cry, when this is all over. We'll have roast goose and a plum tart, and you'll go home to the place you love in America."

She stopped. "But you're freezing. Where have you been, child?"

Shivering in her arms, I told her all of it.

"And you blamed yourself?" she said. "Oh, Genevieve. You couldn't have done better."

I thought of what Herr Albert had said, words that made the terrible trip to the school worthwhile: *not surprised.*

I thought of Aunt Marie. *Any house is rich if you're in it.*

And now this: *You couldn't have done better.*

In spite of this terrible war, in spite of Fürst, in spite of Rémy being missing, in spite of the hunger that cramped my stomach, I felt happiness, like syrup in my chest.

Mémé patted my shoulder and, leaning against the table, got to her feet. "I'll bring our things downstairs again. We'll soak your feet in warm water from the stove and then I'll make a meal from old vegetables I found in the field."

Was she smiling? "Yes, we'll eat before the German returns. There'll be nothing left for him. Not a withered carrot, not a sprig of parsley. What did he say about me? That I was selfish? Indeed, that's what I am."

For that moment, I saw the girl in the painting, her lips curled into that smile.

I wished I had known her then.

# twenty-seven

$\mathcal{K}atrin$ came to the house the day after I'd warned Herr Albert. Neither of us mentioned our argument. She was full of news. "Soldiers burst into school," she said, "looking for something; looking for someone. But they didn't find anything." She raised her shoulders. "And now even Herr Albert has disappeared. The principal has taken over for him. Strange!"

"Yes, strange," I repeated.

It wasn't until the middle of January that my feet healed. Because of those blisters, those aches, Fürst never guessed I was the one who'd warned Herr Albert. Still, I couldn't wait to look for Rémy again. He was out there somewhere. In the cold? Hungry?

One morning the sun shone into the bedroom. I moved my feet under the quilt and felt like myself.

I threw on my clothes and went downstairs. I hadn't

been in school for weeks; no one would miss me for another day, or even another week.

I tried to decide where to go. And then I realized. Rémy would have been afraid to be near the village, where everyone knew him.

I'd chosen the wrong way. Maybe he'd have gone toward the Rhine, even though it was closer to Germany, the area bristling with soldiers.

Before I left, I stood in the kitchen chewing a small knob of cheese, saying good-bye to Mémé. I pumped up the tires. *No blisters this time,* I told myself.

I pedaled along the edge of the road, stopping sometimes, resting and calling softly into the woods. A German soldier driving a truck came by, splashing through puddles, and slowed down, so I wheeled away from him, wondering if he'd stop me. But then he was gone.

I went farther, and as I squinted at the warm sun, I saw the tower.

I thought of the three of us that summer day before the war. *If I could climb to the top—there must be a way—*what had André said? *I'd see the world.*

Maybe I'd see something, even smoke from a fire deep in the woods.

I rode faster. Another truck passed, and a few motorcycles. I paid no attention to them. I passed farmhouses, some of them empty, their owners scattered across France.

My eyes were on the tower as I went closer. The messy storks' nest perched on top, abandoned now; the storks had flown to Spain until spring.

And then I was there.

I dropped the bike in the trees away from the road, so it was almost invisible. I walked around the tower, gazing up, shielding my eyes against the sun.

I looked around, but no one seemed to be nearby. A small door was cut into the back wall of the tower, locked with a thick loop of rusty metal, icy in my fingers. Surprisingly, it came away in my hands. Maybe it hadn't been locked in a long time.

I pulled the door open and peered up at an iron stairway circling to the top. It wouldn't be hard to climb, to see the forest and the small paths meandering through the woods.

Closing the door behind me, I pushed a wooden bolt and locked myself inside.

*Please let me find him.*

The curved stone wall was in front of me,

pockmarked from all the years the tower had stood; the stair railing was so cold I thought my fingers might freeze against it. I pulled off my scarf and wound it around one of my hands. It was an easy climb, the stairway winding gently as it rose toward the top.

Outside, the wind was fierce, the storks' nest larger than it had seemed from below, with sticks hung over the edge of the wall.

I spotted the blue-gray house we'd seen that day, the chestnut tree bare now. From high up, the house and tree were almost like the woodcutter's carved wooden figures.

The woodcutter! Would I ever see him again?

Far beyond that was the bridge over the Rhine. Down below, there was traffic. A line of trucks with the Nazi flag flying in front went by; a motorcycle zigzagged around them. I stood behind the nest, even though I couldn't be seen.

I heard voices, though, blurred in the wind, closer than the road.

Right underneath the tower?

I peered between the branches that lined the storks' nest. Two German soldiers stood there, almost next to the door.

I ducked back, picturing what was happening. I imagined them opening the door, looking up . . .

And I remembered I'd locked it behind me. My hand went to my chest. *Safe, Genevieve, safe.*

I didn't move; I didn't make a sound.

After a moment, I leaned forward again, brushing against the nest, closing my eyes, imagining it toppling, the soldiers looking up.

*Stop.*

The storks had built it firmly against the wind and against me.

One of the soldiers circled a tree. "Hey, Rudy." Then both of them stared down . . .

At my bicycle lying under the trees.

I imagined the rest as I leaned against the wall: they'd brush it off, wheel it away toward the road; one of them would climb on and begin to pedal, the other back on his motorcycle.

When I looked again, that was exactly what had happened. My bicycle was gone, and I was far away from home. Five miles? Almost six?

It was only then that I looked closer at the storks' nest. A few threads of blue wool were caught there. Threads from Rémy's shirt? Yes.

I pulled at them and they came free.

He'd been here, then, and maybe he would come back. But I couldn't wait. I had to get out of the wind, and down below, in the trees, it would be warmer.

*But not safer,* I told myself.

# twenty-eight

$\mathcal{I}$ climbed down the iron steps slowly and pressed my head against the door. Were soldiers outside? Was anyone else nearby?

The door was rock-solid. I couldn't hear anything. I'd have to open it an inch or two. I stood there, my thoughts jumbled. What would I do next? And how would I get back to the farm without a bike?

Cautiously, I pushed back the bolt and opened the door, listening; there were no voices, only the shrill call of a bird. I opened the door farther; I was alone.

And a miracle! My bike was there, leaning against a tree; the rust, the bent spokes, must have sent the Germans away. Who would have wanted that ancient mess?

I did! I was so glad to see it!

I left it there to walk along a narrow path. On either

side, the woods were thick with evergreens and chestnut trees raising their winter arms. Old leaves covered the forest floor.

*Where are you, Rémy?*

The path opened onto a field. Farther on was the back of the blue-gray house, one of the shutters hanging loose.

Had Rémy walked this path?

I circled the field so I couldn't be seen by anyone inside. My feet were soaked; the blisters, which were almost healed, were beginning to rub against my shoes.

At the house a hoe lay on the ground. The house seemed deserted, looking sad and alone. How different from the house we'd seen that warm summer day when André was still here, when Rémy's family was safe . . .

When Rémy was safe.

I stood in the shelter of the trees, ready to bolt. But the windows were blank and bare, one of the panes broken, so I went closer.

On tiptoes, at one of those windows, I looked into the kitchen. The hearth was filled with gray ashes; nothing lay on the counters.

The door opened easily and I went inside. Without

a fire in the hearth, it seemed colder inside than it had been in the field.

I walked through the hall, seeing a bird's nest spilling out from a chandelier, and glanced up the stairs.

And then I heard it, a whisper of sound. Footsteps on the cellar stairs?

I ran back through the hall, into the kitchen and out the door; I closed it without a sound and dashed around the hoe. Had it been a soldier? Or even the owner of the house?

I'd never get to the trees without being seen. Instead, I turned the corner of the house, leaning against the wall, hidden from the door, catching my breath.

Maybe it had been my imagination: a mouse scurrying across the floor, a bird trapped in the upper hallway.

The door opened as quietly as I had closed it. I heard footsteps, but they were running...

Across the field.

I peered around the corner and caught my breath. "Wait! Just wait!"

I stumbled after him. "It's me, Genevieve."

He turned and stopped, his arms out. I ran into him, my arms out too, and we were hugging, laughing. "Only me," I said.

We went back into the house together to sit at the dusty kitchen table, both of us talking at once.

"Your feet clop," he was saying, grinning, and I remembered André saying the same thing when he named Sister.

And I was asking what he'd found to eat.

"The cellar! There was just enough food to stay alive." He shrugged. "The owner must have left quickly. I don't understand why someone else didn't find the jars of vegetables."

I didn't let him finish. We really had no time. I reached out and took his hand, cold from this icy house. "The courier is almost back. Philippe says he'll take you to Switzerland."

He closed his eyes. "So far from Alsace."

"But safe."

Were there tears in his eyes?

"Someone will come for you."

He nodded.

"Oh, Rémy," I said. "Someday, we'll ride bicycles together. We'll . . ."

He leaned forward, touched my cheek. "I know."

I squeezed his hand, then ran across the field,

paying no attention to the puddles that seeped into my shoes.

I straddled that ancient bike. It was cold and the tires were almost flat again.

I prayed to the Alsatian Saint Odile: *Let me do this.*

# twenty-nine

I slowed down when I reached the village, wanting soldiers to think I was coming from school, or visiting friends.

The bookshop was closed, so I went around the back and knocked. Knocked harder. Kept knocking.

And Philippe didn't come.

Where was he?

I tried the door; it was locked, of course.

Madame Jacques stood at her back window. I went toward her. "Have you seen Monsieur Philippe?"

"I have," she said. "He's delivering books to someone. Come in, wait inside, it's cold." She smiled. "The pâtisserie is closed, but there are éclairs upstairs."

I looked over my shoulder.

"Give him ten minutes or so," she said.

I nodded, glad to go into the warmth, and I hadn't

tasted anything as sweet as éclairs in a long time. I followed her upstairs, into her small living room. "Sit, Genevieve. I'll bring in dessert."

She went into the kitchen and called back. "You need a book from Philippe?"

I opened my mouth to tell her I'd found Rémy, but then I stopped. "Yes."

I heard the clatter of plates, and my mouth watered. I hadn't eaten since breakfast. She brought the éclairs in, covered in chocolate icing, forks and napkins on the plate. But she was shivering. "It's a little cold in here." She pointed to the door at one end of the room. "I need a sweater."

I didn't wait. I took the first bite of éclair; it melted in my mouth.

She opened the door halfway; her bed was covered with a patterned blue quilt. And over the bed, I could see the edge of a narrow frame.

How familiar it looked.

I put down my fork.

I thought of Philippe and the gray sweater. Maybe I'd been mistaken about it being André's, but I had to know if I was mistaken about this.

Madame Jacques came out of the bedroom, closing the door behind her, a sweater over her shoulders.

My mouth was dry enough to ask for a glass of water, and she went past me into the kitchen. "I'll be right back," she said.

I was off the couch, opening the door. I heard her footsteps, but still I took the time to look . . .

To see . . .

Mémé's painting on the wall over her bed!

I closed the door and managed to take a few steps. I didn't make it to the couch, but I was almost there, and turned when she came back with the water.

"Thank you." I made myself take a sip, made myself smile.

Fürst must have given the painting to her.

Why?

To thank her for something? For helping him? For helping the Germans?

I gripped the glass to stop my hands from trembling, and sank down on the couch. I'd never be able to eat the éclair.

And then I realized. Where had the eggs come from? The chocolate? The flour?

"Could I . . . ," I began.

She was sitting across from me. "Too bad Claude isn't here. He thinks you're special."

I nodded. "Would it be all right if I took the éclair with me? I need to see if Philippe is back—for the book. And then I have to go home to my grandmother's."

"Of course. Need another napkin?"

I shook my head. "I'm fine." I headed for the stairs, looking back, trying to smile.

I thought of something, and stopped. "Could I ask you? What's your first name?"

"Ah," she said. "It's Suzanne."

"I thought that's what it was." And then I caught myself. "I guess Mémé told me."

I flew down the steps and out the back door. Suzanne.

The one who'd betrayed Rémy and his family?

Maybe the one who'd betrayed my father.

Suzanne the tattletale.

The door was unlocked. I burst inside.

Philippe shrugged out of his coat; he threw his woolen hat on the table, then raised his eyebrows.

I couldn't talk. I didn't know where to begin. I held up my hand.

And then it all spilled out: one word tumbling after another. *The blue-gray house. Rémy there. Waiting. I can show you. Éclairs upstairs. Eggs. Flour. Sugar. From*

*Fürst? The painting. Two girls. Mémé. Enormous bows. Over her bed. Over Suzanne's bed. Yes, Fürst!*

I couldn't breathe, but I'd said it all, and Philippe understood. I could see that.

His hand was on my shoulder, guiding me into a chair. "You saved Albert's life," he said. "Now we know about Suzanne. We could use more like you." He stood over me, smiling. "The American."

"Yes." My voice was strangled.

He went to the small stove and put on a pot of water. *Coffee without coffee.*

"It will end," Philippe said, putting the cup of water in front of me. "Before that, we'll set everything straight. You can count on it. And someday you'll go home. You deserve it."

Home.

Someday.

If only . . .

I sat drinking the water, so hot it almost burned my tongue. I'd never tasted anything so good.

# *thirty*

*Mémé* met me at the door. "I thought you'd never come." She took my cold hands in hers. "I've been waiting..."

"So much to tell you."

Mémé put her finger to her lip. "Fürst has been upstairs for hours," she said. "He has a headache. He thinks you've been nursing your feet in bed all day."

*My feet. Boiling water.* How long ago that seemed.

Sitting in the kitchen, I told her everything, whispering, my head close to hers, even though Fürst could never hear us from upstairs.

"All these years," Mémé said when I was finished.

I wasn't sure if she was talking about Suzanne, or my father, or even the Germans. But I was too tired to think about it anymore.

I didn't even undress. I pulled off my shoes and went

to bed even though it was early. Tomorrow I'd go back to school as if nothing had happened. And Philippe, or someone, would use the map I'd drawn to find Rémy.

I closed my eyes, but thoughts of my father were in my head. I had a father who was grieving when his picture was taken. Now, I knew who'd probably betrayed him, and the rest of the village would know it eventually.

*Her father would have been proud of her.*

Hours later, I felt the light coming from the window on my face, a slim lemon drop of sun coming up over the field, and the sound of Fürst's motorcycle pulling away on the gravel path. I fell asleep again, dreaming that I heard voices in the kitchen.

But at last, I awoke. It was time for school. Time to act as if nothing had happened for all those days, except that I had burned my feet.

Mémé put a small chunk of bread in front of me. I knew it would taste like sawdust. Everyone was doing that now, sprinkling bits of sawdust into the batter so there'd be more to eat. "Put a slice of cheese on top and it will improve the flavor," she said.

I looked at her carefully. Was she crying? "What is it?"

She swiped at her eyes. "Dust. Nothing." She pulled

out the chair across from me. "There's something I want to tell you." Her hands were stretched out.

She unwrapped the bandage around her finger, looked down at her ring, then pulled it off. "You have been a gift, Genevieve."

"I disrupted your house, your life, and all I wanted to do was help."

She took my hand and put the worn ring in my palm.

I looked down at it, a slim gold band, her wedding ring. "Why?" Shocked, I ran my fingers over it. "I can't—"

"There is no one but you." She shook her head. "No, that's not the way I want to say it. I want to give you something of mine. You've brought Gérard back to me with everything you've done. And someday, when I'm gone..."

"Don't say that," I said fiercely.

"I don't mean now." She smiled. "You'll understand soon."

She went to the cabinet and took out a thin chain. "Wear it around your neck. It will remind you of me and Victor, your grandfather." She ran her fingers over it. "We always knew each other, always loved each other.

One half of this farm belonged to my parents, the other half to his. When we were married, it was ours. We'd run through the field, sit on the stone wall, so happy."

She sighed. "He'd always had trouble with his heart, and one day, just after Gérard was born, he died, coming downstairs for breakfast."

She shook her head and threaded the ring into the chain; then I reached for my coat.

"Wear the blue sweater too," she said. "It's cold."

I nodded.

"Oh, something else," she said. "You must stop at Philippe's on the way to school."

"I'm a little late, I think."

"Never mind." Her voice was stern. "You must go there first."

I held up my hand. "All right." I reached forward, pulled her to me and whispered, "It's the best gift I've ever had, Miel. I do love you."

"I'll remember that always." She patted my shoulder. I left the house and ran along the path toward Katrin's, but she had gone ahead.

It really was late.

I reached the village and saw Philippe in the doorway, beckoning to me.

"School," I said. "I have to—"

"Not today."

I glanced toward the road, toward the pâtisserie.

"Come inside, and I'll tell you what we need." He lumbered ahead of me as I followed him inside. "You'll go to the tower and wait for the courier," he said. "You'll help him find the house."

"It's on the road," I said. "Straight past the tower. He won't be able to miss it."

He looked up at the stopped clock. "Ah, American, you have to do this. You'll take my bike and leave it behind the tower."

Philippe was right. I had to do it for Rémy. It was my last chance to say good-bye to him. I nodded. "Yes."

He didn't smile, but there was something in his face; I couldn't imagine what it was. "I want to tell you . . . ," he began. "Such a long time ago. But because you are so like the two of them, your grandmother and your father, I wanted you to know that no one was braver, that no two were ever dearer to me."

Philippe. Tears in his eyes!

"You saved my father, Mémé told me that."

"Ah yes, but she didn't tell you that they saved me as well?"

I shook my head. And I was crying too.

"I had gone alone," he said. "Spying on the garrison, looking for information, and someone saw me in the shadows. I ran through the alley, out into the fields, as they fired after me."

Listening, I couldn't move. I could hardly breathe.

"Shooting me. I lay there bleeding, just as your father had. The two of them came out of the trees, into the line of fire, and pulled me, unable to move, back to where I was hidden. If you could have seen Élise, her hair wild around her face, her face filthy, and your father. Such a wonderful boy."

A boy! I wiped at my eyes.

He smiled, patted my shoulder. "Ah, Genevieve, the memories. But wait, there's a package. Give it to the courier when you see him."

"How will I know who he is?"

He waved his hand. "I've described you to him. He'll be waiting for you." He handed me a box the size of a book, tied with string, and walked to the back of the shop. "A last thing."

I looked up at him.

"Upstairs in my apartment is a small pile of books,

hidden deep in a closet. American books with your name."

"With my name?"

"They wait for you there until . . ."

"But how . . ."

"Albert found them just as the war began and knew they might be dangerous for you. We couldn't bring ourselves to destroy them even though they'd been rain-soaked."

He peered outside to be sure no one was there. "Go." He pointed to his bicycle.

I straddled it and dropped the box in the basket on the handlebars. Head down, I cycled along the alley, passing the boarded-up pharmacy, out onto the road, away from the village and on my way to the tower.

# thirty-one

$\mathcal{I}t$ was a sunny morning with the promise of spring, and Philippe's bicycle was much better than mine.

I raised one hand to finger Mémé's ring on the chain around my neck, feeling its warmth. *If only the Germans were gone. If only I weren't hungry.*

But I was glad for Rémy. In hours he'd be on his way to Switzerland, where there was no war, where he wouldn't have to hide, to look over his shoulder and worry. He'd be with his mother and sister.

Halfway to the tower, a long convoy of trucks began to fill the road. I veered to one side, bumping along under the trees, and waited for the motors to pass. A motorcycle threaded its way around the trucks, and I saw the driver look up.

I held my breath.

He saw me and came toward me.

I was trapped; the trees in back of me were thick and I'd never get the bike through them.

No time to run.

And the box was in the basket in front of me.

What was in it? How could I explain?

"*Fraülein!*" He stopped and gave me the Hitler salute. I looked down at the patches of melting snow, the dark soil.

"What are you doing here?" he asked.

"Going to my aunt's house. Bringing her . . ."

He looked at the box.

I couldn't say food. He might take it. "Bringing her . . . ," I began again. "A book. From my grandmother. An old book."

He stared at me for what seemed to be forever. "You're lying," he said. "You're skipping school for the day. Food in the box?" He flicked his finger at it.

I acted as if I were trying not to smile, as if I really might be skipping school, enjoying a day in the woods.

"I used to do that," he said. "Long ago."

Then he was gone, and the convoy as well.

And I was all right.

I sped along the road, watching the sun rise higher. The courier was waiting. And Rémy.

The tower was in front of me. I pedaled around the side, leaned the bicycle against the stone wall and stood there with the package under my arm.

I saw the courier, carrying a small suitcase. His back was toward me; he was tall, his dark hair curly . . .

"I'm here." My voice was so choked I wondered if he could hear me. "André!"

He turned and I held out the box. "I think I have your sweater."

And then I was crying, not small tears but huge sobs, as André came toward me and wrapped his arms around me. "You're going home, Gen."

*Aunt Marie. The whistle of the train coming into the Higbie Avenue station at night. Oh, home.*

I raised my hands in the air. "How?" And then I saw he was wearing a German uniform.

I stepped back.

"Stolen," he said. "You and Rémy will be my prisoners as we take the train toward Switzerland. We'll walk the rest of the way. There are friends who'll help. Remember the restaurants where I worked. They haven't forgotten me."

I kept shaking my head. "You'll be caught."

He pulled me closer. "I never went home, Gen. I've

been here all this time, bringing people out, because a man named Albert taught me the way."

*Herr Albert.*

"And you left your sweater..."

"Yes."

And then we were laughing, because it was probably the only time in his life he'd left something. He always knew what he was doing. I was the Flyaway Girl, not André.

"I've heard about you and what you've done," he said, his voice catching. Holding hands, we made our way along the small path through the woods to the blue-gray house and to Rémy.

"But Mémé. She'll wonder..."

"She knows," he said. "Someone went to her early this morning and asked..."

The ring! Oh, Mémé!

We smiled at each other.

Going home.

# thirty-two

The three of us sat in the dingy kitchen of the blue-gray house, a torn map spread out on the table.

André traced the route with one finger.

"Strasbourg," he said, "then Colmar. Going south all the time. I have papers for the three of us. It will take weeks, but sometimes we'll be able to sleep in friendly houses, sometimes eat at friendly tables."

I couldn't stop looking at him. He'd grown taller, thinner, and there was the shadow of a beard on his chin.

My brother.

He grinned at Rémy. "The suitcase. Clean clothes."

We waited while Rémy washed himself under a pump in the sink and went into another room to change. We talked, not about Alsace, not about the war. We remembered ice cream sodas at Krisch's, Jones Beach in the summer and stickball on 185th Street outside our house.

I said our father's name, Gérard. We had a father who would have loved us. He did love us. And maybe André was old enough to remember him, to know that.

But there was no time. Rémy was ready.

And so were we.

We walked through the woods, listening to water dripping from tree branches, watching birds fly overhead, going south too.

We stopped dozens of times, to drink from a jug slung around André's shoulder, the sounds of trucks and motorcycles on the road just feet away from us.

I'd be going home to Springfield Gardens, where neighbors could be trusted, where Resistance fighters were far away, where no one had ever heard of a German soldier named Fürst.

I looked at the Vosges Mountains rising up in the west, pictured the village square, the school, the farm, Katrin, Louis, the cat...

And Mémé.

Mémé, who knew I was going home, who'd given me her ring so I'd always have it.

Then Philippe: *You saved Albert's life.*

I stopped, leaning against a tree, the bark thick and damp against my hands.

André turned. "What is it?"

"It's nothing."

But it was something. It was everything.

Mémé would have to plant in the field alone, to be in the farmhouse alone, to explain to Fürst that I was at a cousin's or had run away like Louis.

Gérard's mother.

My grandmother.

I began to walk again, stumbled and caught myself.

"Gen?" André asked.

Philippe's voice in my head. *We could use more like you.*

I shook my head and reached between the buttons of my coat to feel the nubby warmth of the blue sweater.

My Americans would come someday. They'd fight their way across France, and then Alsace, to push the Germans back across the Rhine.

Would I be sitting on a stool at Krisch's ice cream parlor, spooning up a hot fudge sundae?

I glanced at Rémy, who was trudging along. "Wait," I said. "Just for a minute. Let's say good-bye here."

He looked surprised. "We still have a long way to go."

"A long way," I echoed. I put my arms around him. "I'll never forget..." I couldn't finish.

He put his hand on my cheek.

I knew he couldn't talk either.

# thirty-three

$\mathcal{I}$ stepped back. "André?"

We hadn't seen each other in so long, but still he knew what I was thinking. "You don't have to do this, Gen. We'll get you to Switzerland, and then England, and..." He didn't say the word *home*. He waited, his hand gripping my shoulder.

"Mémé," I said. "Philippe. And you, still here."

He leaned over to hold me for a moment. "The Americans will come," he said.

"I'll be waiting for them." I touched his cheek, ran my hand over Rémy's arm and turned back.

"Take Philippe's bicycle," André said.

"What are you doing, Genevieve?" Rémy asked.

"Going back," I said, over my shoulder, trying to smile.

"Flyaway Girl," André called after me.

And Rémy's voice. "No one like her."

I darted through the trees, along the narrow path, my coat snagging on evergreen branches, going toward the tower. The bicycle lay where I'd left it, the metal bars cold and muddy. I wiped them off, and then I was on my way back to the farm.

A freezing rain began, with stinging pellets of ice that quickly settled into a feathery snow.

I'd been so close to going home to America!

What would Mémé say when she saw me? I pictured her in the kitchen, thin as a rail, turning as I opened the door, my boots dripping snow.

Would she be glad to see me? I had to smile. No, her bony hands would go to her mouth. "What have you done this time, Genevieve?"

But I knew her now, loved her now.

I'd go toward her . . .

So I wasn't thinking. I never saw the truck until the horn blasted. The tires screeched as it slid away from me, hitting the rear of the bike.

I was thrown forward into the trees, hitting my head, but up in an instant, leaving the bike, its back wheel twisted, and running, my legs churning, dodging evergreens.

The soldiers were out of the truck, shouting at me, but I didn't stop. I glanced over my shoulder, but I couldn't see more than a foot in back of me.

And they couldn't see me either.

I sank down behind a bare chestnut tree, listening. After a while, I heard the motor start up and the truck pull away.

Still, I waited a long time, taking in huge breaths of the cold air, shivering, before I stumbled over the ruined bike. What would Philippe say? I'd have to leave it.

I'd have to walk.

How far?

It didn't make any difference. Even if it took forever, I was going back to the farm, back to Mémé, back to do whatever I could do for the Resistance.

I sang in an off-key warbling voice under my breath. French songs. American songs. And then . . .

A sound I hadn't heard in a long time.

The clopping of a horse's feet, the rattling of an old cart! I peered through the snow. An old man, wearing a beret, held the reins.

A beret. Amazing. Risking six months in prison.

I caught my breath. It was one of the men from the village, Katrin's grandfather.

I didn't think. I didn't have to think! I ran toward him, slid toward him through the slush, calling.

He pulled up on the reins, turned, and I climbed up on the wooden plank next to him. "Please," I said, "a ride."

He looked across at me, his sparse beard covered with snow. "Katrin's friend, is it? What are you doing out in this weather?"

I opened my mouth, ready to tell him all that had happened. Then I did think. "I was looking for a friend. Martine," I said, instantly making up the name. "I didn't know how far. And then I was lost..." I went on, a long story about the woods, and that I'd have to try again in the spring.

Did he believe me? It wasn't a very good story. I asked him, "And you?"

His story was rambling. Even more unbelievable than mine. I leaned back in the wagon, smiling to myself. Who knew what he'd really been doing?

I closed my eyes, feeling the rocking of the cart. What a long day it had been. And André, here all this time, until the end of the war, just as I was. Not safe, but then none of us were.

I must have slept. I awoke to feel the old man shaking my shoulder. "You're home," he said.

I looked across at the farm, the white field, the stone house, dark with the blackout curtains. Mémé's house. My father's house.

"I can't thank you enough," I said, noticing that the beret was hidden away now.

We grinned at each other. We both knew we had secrets!

I climbed off the cart, and then I was running up the gravel path, banging on the locked door, Louis barking. I couldn't wait now. Banging, as I saw Mémé peer out the window!

*Oh no!* I saw her mouth the words.

She'd be furious. Why not? She was Mémé.

But the door opened, and she pulled me toward her, one hand reaching up to smooth my wet hair. "Ah, Genevieve," she said. "How is it that I knew you'd come?"

We stood there for long moments, Louis at my feet, the cat looking up at me from under the table. I shrugged out of my snowy coat to let it drop on the floor.

Mémé didn't even sigh. I looked into the hallway at the picture of my father. "I'm here," I whispered.

# 1944

# thirty-four

$\mathcal{I}t$ was December again. The sixth Christmas I'd been here. Another long year was behind us. Early in the morning, I went out to the woods, clumping through the thick snow, and cut down a small tree.

Inside, I hung the carved figures on the tree, with the kitchen full of the scent of pine. Mémé watched, so frail now that she spent most of her days knitting on the bench next to the hearth.

I wasn't the same girl who'd turned back from the train station so long ago. I had no time to lose things, to drop books on the counter, socks on the floor. I was up early, to bed late, or sometimes not to bed all night. Besides school and managing to make meals from almost nothing, I worked for Philippe.

I knew now why Rémy loved farming. To work in the field, the soil under my fingers, watching the seedlings that Mémé and I had nurtured grow, was a wonderful feeling. Still, our harvest had been sparse, without potato eyes to plant and only a few seeds for carrots and beans.

I'd learned to be careful of Mémé; I'd slide an extra spoonful of broth into her bowl; I thought she did the same for me.

But we had the radio too!

In June, we'd heard what I'd been waiting for, praying for! The Americans had landed in Normandy.

"Oh, Mémé," I'd said, almost forgetting to whisper. And then I realized. "What will the Germans do to me? I'm American, after all."

She'd put her hand over my mouth gently. "You have a French passport. You chose Alsace. It's not a worry."

I had to believe her. But it would take time before the Americans fought their way toward us, liberating towns as they went, freeing Paris, and then on to Alsace. A long time before I heard those beloved American voices!

*Someday,* I told myself as I entered Philippe's shop on Christmas Eve.

"I have books for you today," he said, speaking in German as soldiers lounged around his counter.

"I love to read," I told him. "You know that."

"That's why there are two! Good German books."

It would be another night without sleep! Two more people in hiding would spend at least one night in our attic space, before I led them to André in the woods!

"What about Rémy?" I always asked when we were alone, and Philippe would shrug. "He's not in Switzerland. He's in the heart of France working for the Maquis. The Resistance."

*Ah, Rémy, stay alive.*

But there was one thing I did that year, one thing, maybe for Gérard, maybe for myself. I crouched in that freezing space upstairs, empty that night, running my hands over his initials, and carved my own initials, *G.M.*, under his, as I talked to him. "I'll never call you Gérard again; I'll never think *my father*. You are *mon père*. You are Papa. I belong to you and you belong to me!"

# SOMEDAY

# thirty-five

That winter was the coldest I could remember, with fierce ice storms and drifting snow. We had no coal left. Mémé and I wore sweaters over sweaters, coats over coats. But the news was exciting. Everywhere people were whispering: *The Americans are coming. They've reached Colmar. The Germans are putting up a fight, but they're retreating, inch by inch.*

And then Fürst was gone, this time forever! And even though our heads were covered with scarves, we heard the guns, the artillery fire.

And one terrible day, we spent in the cellar. But at last there was silence. My war was over. All of it! Mémé and I hugged. Philippe and I hugged. Over!

The animals seemed to sense our joy. Tiger spent time in my lap, and Louis, old now, sat next to Mémé, tail thumping, as she rubbed his ears.

Days later, I went down the path with Katrin, walking slowly, remembering we were eighteen now. Katrin held a sheaf of papers in her hand. "It's time for me to write."

"All about the war," I said as American soldiers came along the road.

"Hey, beautiful," one of them called, and stopped.

"I'm a New Yorker!" I said back, the American words lovely on my tongue.

He looked surprised. I wondered if he believed me.

"Springfield Gardens, Long Island Rail Road, Empire State Building, Jones Beach," I said.

He had to keep going, but he smiled over his shoulder!

I waited for André. I waited for Rémy.

Albert was back, with books under his arm. And even though we waited, hoping, the woodcutter and Rémy's father didn't return; they would never return.

When travel began again, I knew Aunt Marie would come for a long visit. But my place was here with Mémé, to hang her painting in her bedroom, to farm and harvest. And sometime later, I'd go to New York, to visit my beloved Springfield Gardens.

But there was the sound of the horse and cart

coming up the gravel path. André was coming home, bringing Sister back where she belonged!

I ran to meet them, with Louis at my feet, and André held out a red parasol. "For you, Gen!"

How long ago it was that he'd promised me that parasol!

I helped Mémé to the cart, and we smiled as we drove around the village square and the old men in their berets waved.

I thought of Aunt Marie, as I had so many times. *Sometimes people surprise you:* Philippe, and Albert, and Madame Jacques, who had disappeared somewhere . . .

And Mémé.

I couldn't be sorry I'd come to Alsace. I'd never have loved her, never have known Papa.

Philippe was outside now, his hand raised. "Well done, Americans," he called after us.

Later I'd go back to the bookshop for my books. But then André stopped the cart.

Coming down the road . . .

Yes, walking toward us, arms out . . .

I was out of the cart, and we held each other, Rémy twirling me in his arms. "I've been waiting for you," I said.

"It's *someday*," he said as we walked back to the cart together.

I thought of all the things I wanted to tell him. Most of all that I was staying there, that we'd farm together.

Someday!

But he knew that, of course he did.

# Acknowledgments

Heartfelt thanks to Kathy Bohlman and Joan Jansen for their research, to Debbie St. Thomas for suggesting I speak with Marie Kozak, and to Marie for her memories of Alsace.

The Trumbull Connecticut Public Library is home to me; the librarians are warm and knowledgeable. I'm more than grateful to Walter Dembowski, who found two books written in 1915 that were immeasurably helpful in studying the history of Alsace and that even gave me the klapperstein!

It would take pages to thank my editor, Mary Cash! Her thoughts and advice are always tremendously helpful. I thank Terry Borzumato for her support over the years, and Barbara Perris for her careful copyediting. Special thanks to Becca Standlander for the beautiful artwork and to Kerry Martin for the wonderful art direction and design.

When I was young, I longed for a big family, and now I have it. I especially want to mention our newest member, Haylee Elizabeth, who calls me Mimi.

Nothing would be possible without my husband, Jim, my best friend. I think of my son Jimmy with every word I write, his love for books, for family, the joy he gave me and others.

George Nicholson bought my first book at Viking and became my agent. He was a source of advice and encouragement for my writing life. I miss him every day.